SAMUEL NOWAK

CAITLYN J. BOLTON

Samuel Nowak

The following is a work of fiction, any names, characters, places, or incidents are a product of the author's imagination. Any resemblance to persons, living or dead, is coincidental.

Copyright © 2020 by Caitlyn J. Bolton

All rights reserved. No part of this publication may be reproduced, scanned, or transmitted in any form, digital or print, without the author's written permission.

First published by Caitlyn J. Bolton 2020

Credits

Cover Art by Ryan Queen

ISBN-9798637478002
ISBN-978-1-71699-826-3

aworldinpages.blogspot.com

Start with what is right rather than what is acceptable.

- Franz Kafka

CHAPTER ONE

Throughout my years on this earth I have struggled and fought my own mind. It now appears to me a separate evil entity, that has a desire to pull me from all hope that occurs in my life. I have allowed it to beat me, and now I reside here, among the sick and the vulnerable, waiting for the moment that I shall cross over to the next world from this. The reason that I write this, is so my reader may learn from my mistakes and lead a more fulfilling existence than what I have. I once had a goal for my life, like any other human on this earth, but I was too weak to fight those obstacles that stood in my way, and I urge you, dear reader, to not do as I, for it will end you sooner than death. So, my dear reader please continue on as I tell you my story.

I was born in Prussia and spent the first four years of my life in my native country, a time when I of course don't remember much, but from what I was told when I was old enough, we had nothing but good times there. The reason we left, according to my dad, was because like most at this time, he became so intrigued by America, Canada and New Zealand, that were advertised as lands of opportunity, that he decided to take us on that perilous boat journey to England. To get to America we first needed to stop in here. My dad,

Bart, hoped to gather enough money working in this country to make that final move to the land of opportunities. At only four years old I do not remember much about the journey, but what I do remember and was later told, I believe it was better that I was too young to fully understand the extent of the horrors that occurred during this time. People got sick on the journey across, and there was no medicine nor doctor to cure them. My mum tried to shelter me from the details, but my dad thought, that as a man in the making, I should be fully aware of the horrors that God challenges us with from time to time. He always blamed my mum for my softness, or to use his words, for his "pansy of a son", he thought he could cure me by telling me the horror stories about men and woman killing and humiliating each other. I took him telling me these stories the wrong way as a child. I thought that he was opening the door to us bonding by sharing tales of evil horrors, but instead when I showed him one I made up on my own he tore it up, threw it at me and called me pathetic, "only weak men write stories!" he would say in his usual and unchangeable, mocking tone, "are you a boy?" he would ask again mockingly, which confused me as to whether or not I should answer. When he repeated this question louder so Alex could hear, she would giggle, and I knew I had to answer as a way to save my childish pride.

When I was older, my mum told me that conscription was the reason my dad wanted to leave Prussia, he did not want to support a government he felt were corrupt, especially if that meant risking his life. His own father disowned him after this point. Like Bart, his dad had certain ideologies of what a man is, and in the eyes of my grandfather a man would willingly fight for his country, whether they supported the government or not. Before this point they were close, best friends almost.

Bart aspired to be like his dad his whole life, a lawyer with a healthy, happy family and beautiful wife and for the most part he had that. When I was born my grandfather loved me like I was his own son, as my mother told me. She said, in her gentle loving tone as she always had, "I think your father got jealous a little. Your grandfather obsessed over you more than he ever did with your father, but all grandparents are like that with their first grandchild."

"What about Uncle Oskar? Does he not have a family?" I remember asking my mother when I was seven and she was telling me about Prussia. We were never close with my Uncle Oskar, my father refused to speak with him for reasons that are still unknown, but my mother spoke of him occasionally when either me or Aleksandria asked about "the old country" as we would call it. "Uncle Oskar hasn't settled down with a wife yet" she would say bitterly, "so no he does not have a family yet." this is usually where we'd end the conversation. There was something about my uncle Oskar that fed my mother's fury, something so deeply rooted that we, even as adults never understood.

Before we continue, I feel it is necessary to specify the jobs my mum and dad had. My mother was a nurse and my father a lawyer, both respectable positions in society and left us with a very comfortable lifestyle. This also meant that we had little struggle in securing tickets for the boat that would first go to Great Britain. My father hoped to stop here for only a little while to pick up his wealth before we made the official move to America. We arrived at a dock in the East end of London, which, for most immigrants became home however my father hated the city and instead wanted to move into a smaller town where there would be a hospital for my mother to work in and a law firm for himself. But of course, he also wanted a highly rated school nearby so his two children could get the best education they could. Although it was supposed to be a temporary move, my dad was one who always thought of the future and wanted to be prepared for anything, and we would soon be thankful for this habit that at the time we thought unnecessary. We ended up in Lewes, not too far from London, it is situated in East Sussex, which was an hour train journey from London. For the first few weeks we were burning through our savings we had brought with us, in a comfortable and cosy inn, until thankfully my dad secured a position in a law firm just outside of Lewes. Once he got his first wage, we were off and into a proper home, one slightly bigger than our old home in Prussia. One thing that never changes about the careers my mum and dad had taken is the wealthy wages they would get every month, no matter the currency or the country. Our home was in the west side of Lewes. It was a beautiful Georgian house which had a majestic garden. It had three main bedrooms, a nursery, a dining room, a sitting-room, a kitchen, and two bathrooms. Not long after we moved in my mother had secured her own position as a nurse at Lewes Victoria Hospital, before she started however she made sure her home was looking its best so she spent most of my father's wages decorating and buying the furniture for our new home. For any readers who may be unfamiliar with society during 1886, traditionally at this time a woman would not need to work, for their husband would earn enough money to provide for her and the children, and my father did earn enough for all of us but my mother had very expensive tastes so she worked to fund that. For the first while my father felt it appropriate that we waited until the start of the next school year before we started our educational career in primary school, but then he realized we would still be behind the other children regardless due to the difference in the curriculum, instead he hired a private tutor and full time nanny until we were ready to start secondary school. I remember our nanny with such reluctance. Her name was Ms Maxwell, she was petite, with gentle features. When she was around my mother and father, she appeared to be angelic and kind, a perfect disguise for the monster that lay underneath. It appeared that only Alex and I would be exposed to the devil that hid inside this fiend of a woman. She was my father's personal choice as a nanny, out of all the woman he interviewed he chose the most attractive yet deceiving, his intentions were, to anyone with a mature mind at the time, clear but my mother turned a blind eye to this action.

Once Satan's servant was properly settled into the role, and my mother was happy with how our new home was looking my mother and father felt comfortable leaving us alone with the witch, not only during the days they were at work but sometimes when they wanted a day to be on their own. Ms Maxwell had strict rules and for some time I believed my mother and father had no idea of the types of punishments she would give. I would have continued believing this if I had not encountered moments where my father and Ms Maxwell were left alone and there seemed to be an intense fondness between them, that wouldn't be there if there were secrets between them. Or at least that is what my childish mind believed. There was one day that Ms Maxwell had crossed a line in my mind, but you will soon see my father had different moral standards. I had just turned eleven at this point and Alex was nine, since we did not have any friends our age and were seldom allowed outside, we had to make do with what we had. We were running round the dining room table playing a game of tag, when Alex accidentally struck the cabinet that my mother stored all her ornaments and prize crockery. At first it shook a little, for how hard can a nine-year-old girl really hit a large wooden cabinet? We both held our breaths until the fatal moment when an ornament had fell from the cabinet and smashed on the floor. And of course, this got that old witch's attention. She rushed to the dining room and saw us both with our jaws on the floor and our eyes filled with terror. At first she looked at me on the other side of the room and then with a flash of fury she darted over to Alex, grabbed her arm and with no word of warning she struck the poor child with the back of her hand on her face, the strike was so hard that she fell to the floor and immediately started bawling. At this point you're probably wondering what I did at this moment and to my shame I must admit I did nothing to help my sister but instead ran upstairs to the nursery with fear and hid from Ms Maxwell. My sister would soon follow with a new bruise on the side of her face. I felt wracked with guilt but at the same time I was relief it wasn't me.

My mother always came home before my father; Bart felt it his duty as the man of the household to earn the most money for his family. When my mother got home, we were both in the nursery in absolute silence, we could hear the sweetness of our mother's voice filling the home as soon as she entered, a sound that brought my poor sister to tears. She went to the sitting room with intentions of relieving Ms Maxwell, but Ms Maxwell had told her immediately what had happened to the ornament in the cabinet with a sense of childlike excitement that nether myself or Alex could have ever expected from her, "The girl, Alexandria, she knocked into the cabinet so hard it broke one of your lovely plates. Well I sent her up to her room and Samuel went with her and I haven't seen the two since." My mother, as we could tell from the tone of her voice, was not entirely bothered about it, "oh accidents happen, Abigail, they are only children after all," we would hear her say faintly from the nursery and when Ms Maxwell left she came up to find myself and Alex on the floor, Alex with her head in her hands bawling. "It's okay" she said with her angelic voice, "accidents happen" she said as she kneeled on the floor and reached over to Alex to hug her. The difference between my mother and Ms Maxwell, was my mother's gentle features and angelic voice was no disguise. I believe to this day that there was no darkness hiding in my mother whatsoever, I do not believe she could have had a bad thought in her whole life. Alex was too afraid to lift her hands from her face but as she felt the warm embrace of our mother and the sweet smell of her perfume had started to flood the room, she hugged her back as tightly as she could. At this point my mother saw the fresh bruise on her face and panicked, "Alex what has happened to your face?" she said while her face turned white with the shock, but then she calmed down and tried to find a reasonable explanation, "Were you and Sam play fighting again?" I was almost insulted that my mother's immediate assumption was I did that to my poor sister, but at the same time I thought I was just as bad for leaving her afterwards and hiding in the nursery. "It was Ms Maxwell!" I said, quickly as my heart raced inside my rib cage with fear and excitement, "What?" my mother said in disbelief, it looked like she believed what I was saying but was shocked at the words, she gazed down at her infant cradled in her arms, Alex nodded, then my mother assured us of our safety, "I promise you both that woman will never step foot in this house again, I will speak to your father tonight about it." she looked back down to Alex who was sobbing quietly, "I'm sorry this happened," and then she kissed her forehead, squeezed my shoulder and left the room. It wasn't long before she called us down for dinner and then we sat in the sitting-room as she read us a story.

When my father came home that night, she expressed her concerns about Ms Maxwell and I padded down a couple steps in my bear feet, trying to be as quiet as I could as I was supposed to be in bed. I heard half the conversation, "I do not trust her around our children anymore Bart, I would think you as their father would share my concerns"
"She made a mistake, we shall speak to her and let her know that we do not approve of this kind of punishment, there's no need for drastic measures, the child only has a bruise not a broken bone." "Bartosz Nowak! That is not any *child* that is your daughter! I will not stand by as someone abuses my children, if you do not release her I will take the children and leave tomorrow." there was an intense silence that I could feel all the way from the sitting-room to my eavesdropping position on the stairs, then my father replied, "Very well, she will be gone tomorrow, but you will need to take some time off while we look for a replacement." his reply was almost spiteful. I waited a while to hear if there would be anything else said but after a while, I felt confident that the conversation was concluded.

The next morning my mother woke us up and got us ready for the tutor coming for our daily lesson.
I was not surprised to see her as I had heard the conversation about Ms Maxwell, but Alex was both surprised and delighted. My lessons that day felt like they flew by. I had no idea how much I dreaded Ms Maxwell's presence until I noticed the change in the atmosphere of the house and how clear my head felt. The summer was creeping in and I would soon be sitting my end of term test which would determine my maths and literature levels for when I went to secondary school. I felt confident in my work

throughout the year, so I was not worried about it. After our lessons, our mother didn't say anything about Ms Maxwell, and we didn't ask. It felt a lot more peaceful and comfortable in the home now that she was gone but something didn't feel exactly right. Although Ms Maxwell was gone and what I heard from the conversation between my mother and father last night was civil, to my childish naivety, my mother still seemed to be distant, like something was distracting her. I wanted to ask but I felt that I had no business sticking my nose in adult problems, and a part of me feared the curiosity and thought it better to stay ignorant. We sat with our mother in the kitchen as she prepared our lunch. While she worked away, she asked us questions about our lessons and our hobbies, as she worked so often that she didn't get the chance to get to know us too well. "How are your lessons going?" she asked us both, Alex told our mother about how she was enjoying her drawing lessons the most and she told us how she would much like to be an artist when she grew up, I replied next, "I think I'm doing well, I like literature the most, but I think I would like to be a lawyer like dad when I grow up" she stopped chopping the vegetables but did not look at me, as I reflect I think she was disappointed in my answer and maybe she knew how this path was going to end. "Oh" she replied awkwardly, "I'm sure your dad would love that, you should tell him when he gets home" I sat quietly. I was afraid to tell my father anything as it seemed no matter what I said it disappointed him.

Although Ms Maxwell was horrible part of my childhood, she struck a great mine of inspiration for my stories. When dinner was over that day, I begged my mother to excuse me from the table early so I could write down my many ideas for monsters. I was never a great artist unlike Alex and I didn't want to waste my time trying to portray these images with my terrible skills, so instead of drawing I used my words to form the visions in my mind and tried to portray my ideas as clear as possible without using pictures. I then picked one of my best creations and put it into a story which the next morning I showed to my mother and she read while I was at the tutor. "Samuel this is amazing for someone your age. So much detail and the story are so interesting. Where did you get the idea for this?" I never revealed my true source for my inspiration, from fear I would be scolded for being disrespectful, "I dreamt it two nights ago, and I couldn't stop thinking about it, so I had to write it down."

"Well it is looking like we have the next Shakespeare in our house" she said to Alex who begged to read it herself, but she was too young to read, and my handwriting would have been too hard to understand. As a solution my mother decided to read it to her after dinner and then she told me she would show it to my father when he got home from work. Although my previous experience with showing my father my stories was negative, I felt confident with this one as I truly believed it was good enough for him. As we all waited for his return, I can remember pacing the sitting-room with excitement. My mother urged me to sit down but I couldn't bring myself to obey, there was too much energy bursting through me. This day so happened to be the day he was to stay late. So late that my mother gave up waiting for him and sent us both to bed without seeing him at all. The disappointment I felt is indescribable it was so powerful, but my mother promised to show it to him anyway and said he would talk to me about it when he got home the next day. But as a child it was like Christmas to me. I couldn't wait until tomorrow I had to hear how proud he would be of me right then and there. So I waited up until I heard him walk through the door, first my mother made him a cup of tea and his supper, so I took this time to sneak to the top of the stairs so I could hear every word. "what's this?" I heard him say flatly, I was hoping, almost praying that he would be more enthusiastic when he found out it was a story I did. "Read it honey, Sam did" there was a brief but intense moment of silence that made my heart drop to the pit of my stomach. "Men don't write stories. You will not encourage this Nadia. The boy must become a man, he can't do that by writing fairy tales at this point my heart felt as though it went through the floor. "It's not a fairy-tale, Bart, it's a horror story, it's about a monster-"

"I will hear no more!"

"Bart! he's your son!"

"He is a man! Or at least he should be, I will have no more of this, he needs to learn the way of the world and writing stories won't get him far. If it was Aleksandria it would be different, she doesn't need to worry about a career as long as she can find herself a real *man* with a good *real* career. Not this nonsense. You will not encourage this any further Nadia." I heard the room fall silent and I padded back to my room. Sleep would be a stranger to me that night while the pain in my chest took its place.

During the summer, my mother and father had hired our neighbour as a nanny, she was in secondary school herself, in her final year, and was glad to earn some extra money so she could go out with her friends during her days off. Her name was Claire, she lived with her widowed mother in a home that her father had left to them after his death. She had the dream to be a nurse, but hoped one day the suffragettes would make enough progress so women could become doctors, I learned all of this from overhearing her conversations with Alex who was too young to understand a word, but Claire thought it was her duty to express how important it was that Alex took advantage of our father paying for her to have the same education as me, which, during this time, not many fathers whether they were rich or poor would do the same for their daughters. Claire's father wanted to see his wife and his daughter strive in the world after his departure, so he made it his dying wish that his daughter would go on to study whatever she wished. Claire was a lovely young woman, even at her young age you could see she was ready for motherhood by the way she looked after us. She had a childlike nature that was mixed with the right amount of responsibility that made her a great friend and a great nanny. Although I was eleven and still a child, I felt the need to impress Claire. I was convinced that one day I would marry her. Silly now to believe that I would have a chance with such a woman, even if we were the same age, I would have never been able to provide the lifestyle she would have been comfortable with, that she deserved.

Claire would play with us in the garden when the weather permitted and then, with her own money, took us to the chip shop for dinner when our mother was working late. On days that the weather wasn't the best she would create a treasure hunt for us if she was over when we were still in bed and the winner would get to pick the book she would read for us in the sitting-room later on that day. A lot of the time she and Alex would be playing with the doll house in the nursery which I didn't mind. I did much prefer being alone and if I ever did want company, they would both be more than happy to include me into another game. One morning Claire had come over with fresh pastries from the bakery and we had them with our lunch. It was only ten minutes before my mother was supposed to leave for work and this for Claire was late, "I wonder where she is?" my mother asked out loud, but I don't think she was asking us, "She'll be here soon" I said as I went to join my mother at the window and that was when we saw Claire speeding towards the house on her bicycle, the pastries from the bakery in the basket at the front, my mother released a breath she must have been holding for a while. She rushed to go meet Claire at the door, worried she was going to be late for work. Claire was already apologising and explaining herself as my mother opened the door, "I am so sorry Miss, the line at the bakers was out the door and I wanted to get some sweet pastries for Sam and Alex for after lunch. I was just handed the parcel when I saw the time so I rushed over here as soon as I could. I hope you aren't late! I hope I'm not keeping you-"

"My goodness, Claire," my mother cut in with a laugh that brightened the sky, "I've still got ten minutes before I have to leave you're still on time, I was just worried because you are usually here a lot earlier, and please there is no need for formalities, call me Nadia," Claire's face had relaxed and they both ended up laughing about Claire's over reaction. The pastries were delicious, they always were from that local bakery, and I'm sure Claire would have agreed that they were worth the stress she went through getting them back on time.

There was one night when my mother and father were supposed to be working late so they paid Claire extra. But out of the blue my father had returned home a few hours before my mother was due home and he paid Claire her promised extra wage and relieved her of the night shift. Not long after he had been home, I heard a knock at the door. With all my childish curiosity, I quietly glided down the stairs to see the wicked Ms Maxwell, speaking with my father in the dead of night. At first, I believed that she may have showed up to get her position as a nanny for us back, but something seemed odd for her to be here at the late hour it was. Then it was all made clear, "I knew it wouldn't take

long for you to bring me back," she said to him, I half expected my father to slap her for the attitude she was giving him but he didn't, "don't get to full of yourself now Abigail, I have a wife, I don't need you,"
"No? Well why am I here?" she reached up to my father's face with her own and kissed him with such passion it gave me chills and made me feel such incredible shame, as if it was my morals I was defying. He pushed her away at first and then grabbed her face hard, "don't get smart with me woman,", I couldn't see her face clearly, but I could tell she was frightened of him. She released herself and stood in front of him with her arms folded. This would have been enough to frighten me or Alex into submission, but there didn't seem much that frightened my father. As strange as I felt, I couldn't look away and there was some sense of excitement bubbling within me that I tried to suppress so I could ignore it. He pulled her back and then with what looked like one rough grab, guided her to the sitting-room. I followed. I do not understand why but I did, it felt like I was being possessed and the entity wanted me to witness the crime first-hand. I hid behind the door to the sitting-room and peered into see our old nanny on top of my father. Horrified I ran back upstairs and to my bed, but I could not sleep that night, instead I sobbed hard into my pillow and begged for my mother to come home and vanish the evil in the house.

The next morning, I planned to tell Claire and ask her to tell my mother, but my anxiety grew fast and regardless she wasn't there. In fact, both my parents were at home. At first, I thought it was because my mother found out about Ms Maxwell, but both were smiling from ear to ear, holding hands on one of the couches in the sitting-room. Only my mother's smile seemed genuine, however. When both myself and Alex were awake and, in the sitting, -room they told us they had some exciting news. The four of us would soon be the five of us. My mother was pregnant.

CHAPTER TWO

Adding a third child into the mess of a family we had seems to me now the biggest mistake my parents made, it put a hold on our plans to move to America any time soon, which my father would express to me how disappointing it was to him whenever we were together. Summer ended quickly once we discovered my mother was having another child. Her morning sickness became too much, and she had to take leave from her work until after the baby was born. My father was not happy about it but he had to accept it as she was about to give him a new child, one which my father hoped and prayed to be a boy, I have no doubt he was hoping to replace me with a son he could raise to be more "manly". As much as we loved our mother and enjoyed her company, during her pregnancy she was completely unbearable. I think it was the morning sickness that caused it, she hated being out of work as well, she loved what she did, she loved helping people.

My last test put me in the highest level of literature and an average level of mathematics which again did not please my father, he saw English as a waste of time as it wasn't as challenging as mathematics, but my mother was proud of my marks regardless. "You should be so proud of yourself Sam. You'll be in the top classes for almost everything. But don't worry about maths, I was never good at either, and neither was my mother or father. We were all much better at literature" this was at the earlier stages of her pregnancy of course when she was only dealing with morning sickness and nothing that was soon to come. I was very nervous for my first day. The night before I went to bed as early as I could after I ate. But even at that I could not sleep, whether it was excitement or nerves, the latter being more convincing, my body would not rest. I tossed and turned and eventually gave into pacing the room until I tired myself out, which took a long time.

My first day was, needless to say, a shock to the system, and thanks to my night spent worrying about it, it proved to be very exhausting. We had to swap classrooms and teachers with every individual subject, the horrid busy halls which had the most intimidating paintings of scenes from the bible became sickeningly familiar after the first change. The classrooms were cold, and the chairs were uncomfortable and as much as I like to pretend it didn't bother me, no one sat with me unless there were no more chairs left next to their friends. Until Literature which is where I introduce the man that sits here with me now, a man who has done nothing but stay with me through each wrong decision I've made. I do not feel as though I am deserving of being acquainted with a man such as Oliver McCarthy, however you will discover those reasons quite soon. Oliver was from a Scottish family, although he was not an immigrant himself, meaning he was born in this country, he still developed his family's strong accent which unfortunately for this time made him stand out and others avoid something simple as eye-contact. If you were not familiar with the politics at the time you would think this innocent child had some horrible disease that spread through any form of socialising.

Even at this first brief encounter, my heart went out to him. Although, I, myself struggled with making friends, part was by my own choice and not prejudice. I sat in the front row of the class; our tables were in pairs.

When he walked in, he wore his anxiety, unintentionally it seemed, on his face. I wanted to tell him not to worry as I felt the same way and he could consider me a friend, but due to my own fear I held back and made the poor boy make the first move. He observed the classroom to see the groups that were shutting him out without being aware that he was alive. There were no seats available other than the ones in the front row, but as he contemplated sitting alone and sitting next to me more people came in and filled the front row leaving the seat next to me the only one available. He edged cautiously towards it; I kept my head to the table afraid to make eye-contact for whatever reason I had. I could feel his nerves fill the atmosphere and selfishly I couldn't stop myself from resenting him a little for making me feel just as nervous. He took a deep breath in preparation as he stood in front of me and he pointed to the empty seat next to me and asked if he could sit there. As I looked up to reply I could see him facing the rest of the room waiting for someone to make fun of him. I told him he could before someone else came in and took it from him. As he moved round to the seat his nerves surrounded me and I was plagued with them. He pulled out the chair softly trying to prevent the loud and obnoxious noise of the chair scraping against the wood flooring and sat down taking out his pen and a notebook and waiting patiently but tense for the teacher to arrive. As much as I felt sympathetic towards him, I couldn't stand him for the time that we waited for our teacher to start the class due to how his nervousness consuming me.

When Mr Roberts, our teacher, had finally made it to the class, I breathed a sigh of relief. I glanced over at the boy next to me from the side of my eye, worrying he had heard me and I tried not to make it obvious that I was looking at him, but he felt my stare and he looked back at me the same way. I laugh now thinking how childish we acted, I think that if I knew that we would have the friendship we have now I would have been less closed to conversation. When Mr Roberts had introduced himself, he went over the pieces we would be covering in the class. One of the first books we were to read was going to be *A Study in Scarlet* by Arthur Conan Doyle, my heart jumped at the prospects, he then revealed we would also be going over several Shakespeare pieces, which I feel no shame in expressing how very excited I was to get to that part of the course. After discussing the course content, he left us to get to know each other as a way to fill up the time we had left. I was surprised at this moment as the shy boy who sat next to me had immediately began the conversation. "My name's Oliver" his thick Scottish accent told me why he was being shut out by the rest of our school, he held out his hand waiting for a handshake. "I'm Sam" I replied and shook his hand. When I moved to England with my family, I managed to hide my Prussian accent thanks to the tutors and Ms Maxwell, I found it strange that at this point in his life Oliver, being born in this country, hadn't adapted an English accent himself. It wasn't until I met his family that it all made sense. "what do you like to do when you're not at school?" he asked, "I like to write sometimes, other than that I don't do much, I don't know anybody around here. What about you?"
"I don't know anybody either, I was home-schooled before this, it's just me and my brother's but they all have their own houses now. When they come over though we play football down at the park." he spoke so

enthusiastically it amazed me and inspired me to express the same enthusiasm. But with my sleep deprived stated that proved to be impossible, "What park?"
"The one just across the road from the school. Haven't you been?"
"No, me and my sister usually play indoors, or in the garden." he looked at me shocked, "You have a garden?" he asked, eyes wide, "Yes, don't you have one?"
"No, your family must be pretty rich to have a garden. Is it a big one?" he was utterly dumbstruck at the idea of someone he now sits with being wealthy enough for a luxury I always took for granted.
"Um, I don't know, it's not as big as the one my parents had in Prussia, but I've only seen that one in pictures. Why don't you have a garden?"
"Mum said she would rather us have an education than a fancy house, she said once we have that we can get a good job and a big house if *we* wanted." he sounded so disappointed with this and I couldn't blame him,
"Maybe I can come over to your house and we can play football in your garden?" I felt bad for what I had to respond with, but I was still taken aback with his forwardness, "I can't, my mum's not well right now and my dad's always working."
"Oh, well maybe when she's better then?" I just nodded, I wasn't sure if this was normal, to openly invite yourself to someone's home after just meeting them.
"What do you do when your brothers aren't visiting?" I asked him, "Not much, I like to write sometimes as well, but I mostly help out my mum with the chores since my only other two siblings are only three," the way he spoke about his family was so intriguing, he carried a strange sense of pride in his tone that I had never heard before. "You have a really big family," I said, not sure how else to reply, "Yeah but my big

brothers have their own houses now and they only come back on Sundays so really it's just me and the twins."

Our conversation continued on until break, and we met again at lunch which was a relief for we soon discovered that we would be excluded from every friend group in the dining room. We discussed our interests and hobbies further. He revealed to me he liked to write poetry and he was mostly inspired by Shakespeare but also Oscar Wilde. I told him that I to, took inspiration from Shakespeare, but not for his poetry but his plays. I enjoyed writing horror stories, most of all ones that involved ghosts and vampires. I read Dracula by Bram Stoker as it had just been published and Frankenstein by Mary Shelley which I was recommended by the bookseller who sold me Dracula. I tried Jane Austen and Willkie Collins, also some Charles Dickens. I liked Willkie Collins, but the others weren't able to keep my interest, this was probably due to the fact that neither Austen nor Dickens wrote in the genre I was interested in. From this revelation of each other's shared passion for creativity we became bonded and our conversations were endless. "My brother Creighton loves Dracula, but I'm not too much into novels, I just prefer poems," I knew the moment I found out he was interested in writing that he was a poet, I think it was his passion when he spoke about the author's he was reading that exposed him. "I haven't really read many poems, the ones I did read I didn't like, I think I prefer longer stories"
"Poetry is more than just stories, it's emotion and senses all wrapped into a word, accessible to anyone with the ability to read. Can you imagine being able to feel what someone else was feeling at a single moment in time."

"Oh, you are definitely a poet." I laughed, "but you can get the same thing from a novel and more, you can enter a whole other world and leave at any time you like, what could be better than that?" we debated from this point until we found ourselves at the end of the first day of secondary school and we were standing outside of the school gates. "My house is down this way" he pointed to his left, "Would you like to join us for tea?" "I can't I have to get back home to help my sister with mum, maybe tomorrow?"
"Yes! I hope your mum starts feeling better. Has she got the flu? My brother Cromwell had the flu last year during the winter. It was awful, he had to stay with us because Penny was too scared that Cory was going to catch it and wouldn't be able to fight it since he is so young. He recovered pretty quickly though." I took from this that Penny was Cromwell's wife and Cory were their son, I don't think Oliver remembered that I only met him that day, so I wasn't exactly on a first name basis with his family. "She's not got the flu, she's having a baby, but the baby is making her ill."
"Oh," he looked at me confused, lost for a response, I felt uncomfortable and stood for a moment thinking of a way to divert the topic to something else, "Once she has the baby she'll be better, my mum was sick a lot with the twins but after they were born she got much better," I appreciated his attempt at assuring me for a better outcome. We then said goodbye and we went our separate ways home.

When I returned home, I couldn't wait to tell everyone about Oliver, my father included. I took our friendship as my biggest achievement up until this point. However, when I returned home that excitement faded. My mother was in bed, for she felt incredibly ill while I was away. Alex was left
to entertain herself in the nursery and my father was

still at work. The contrast between being with Oliver to being with my family was extreme. While I was with Oliver, we would play all different sorts of games and he taught me to play football, although I wasn't very good and found myself sitting out more times than actually joining in when he was playing with the other boys from our school. This was not the last day that would be like this. My mother became so ill that she couldn't leave bed and Alex had to take time away from her lessons to care for her, after all my father was not going to take any time off himself or pay for a nurse regardless if he had the money for it. Every night I would come home from the liveliness of Oliver's company to silence and a lifeless home. Alex did her best to keep the house clean for she knew our father would not be happy otherwise. I tried to help her out as much as I could with the cleaning and caring for our mother, but I had a lot of work to do for school and I prioritised that over anything else. Poor Alex, at only ten years old became a nurse to our mother, I believe it ended her childhood sooner than it should have for after this point she was never the same. She became so serious and dreary, the life seemed to fade from her eyes and complexion. I didn't notice it at the time, but I now know that this was the time that I lost my little sister.

After the first week of school, Oliver and I felt we had settled in enough to our new schedule and decided to join some clubs. We tried almost everyone and rounded it down to our favourites after that week had finished. We both liked the debate club and found ourselves competing against each other most of the time and continuing those debates all the way to school gates. It was of course in good spirit and I felt being able to disagree so strongly and being able to discuss it with each other only strengthened our friendship. Oliver had

convinced me to join the football team but only after I made the compromise that he would join the chess club. It ended up that I never stuck at football and he never stuck at chess so when either one of us were at one of those clubs the other would wait behind so we could leave together. One day after football practice Oliver had come out with ripped trousers and a huge cut on his knee. He didn't seem phased by it but if it was me, I would be in a great panic of my mum seeing my ripped trousers. "Isn't your mum going to be angry about your trousers?" I asked him as we began to walk out the school, he scoffed, "Of course not, it happens all the time to my dad and my brothers when they were younger, my dad calls it an occupational hazard." I didn't think his dad's occupational hazards were the same as the ones caused by football, but I didn't question it. I learned quite quickly that Oliver and his family were a bit different from other families. The next day Oliver was wearing the same trousers that were subtly sewn back together by his mother. I would never have known if he hadn't pointed it out so proudly as we walked to class. "See, I told she was fine with it." he said smugly, "What are you on about?"
"My trousers, my mum stitched them up and washed them for me all in one night," I looked down at them trying to find the evidence, "she's really good at stitching, my dad would have no shirts by now if she wasn't," he laughed and I joined in not sure in the beginning if it was a joke.

When things got worse with my mother, I decided to confide my burden in Oliver, instead of the judgement I expected he invited me to his house to have dinner with his family. He assured me I would not be imposing as his older brothers and their families would also be coming over, as they did every Sunday, and his mother loved to cook. Needless to say, I was flattered with his offer as it was one, I thought I would never be given, and I took him up on it. My mother was nearing the end of her pregnancy, and although she was still sick and was not able to get out of bed, I did feel the need to get her permission before going to Oliver's house, especially because I had never been before and I wasn't entirely sure of where it was. "Who is Oliver?" she asked me as she sat up in her bed sipping the tea Alex had just made her. "He is my friend, I wanted to tell you about him, but it never seemed that there was an appropriate time since you have been ill"

"I'm so sorry Sammy, I have become ill at such an awful time, I missed your first day at school and now you're telling me about your first friend. I haven't been a very good mother to either of you," she looked over at Alex who was standing cautiously in the doorway, then she beckoned her forward and gestured us to sit with her on the bed with her. "Once this new baby comes, we'll get back to being a proper family again, I promise." she nestled us into her, and then continued, "You can go to your friend's house for dinner, but you will need to find your own way to get there because your father will be at the firm, is his house close by?" "Of course, my plan was to meet Oliver at the school and then we will walk together," I lied partially, I didn't exactly know how close it was, but I was meeting Oliver at the school and we would walk together. That Sunday I made my way to his house in the early afternoon. Little did I know at the time, this would be the first dinner of many.

Oliver's family were a group of strange and wonderful people, each were equally enthusiastic and incredibly welcoming. It was a delight to be around them. Every Sunday they had dinner as a family and I was treated as one of them, from the first moment I walked through the door. I found this a strange routine as we had never done so ourselves, but it was an incredible experience. When I first met the twins, they were shy for a while, mostly Nolan, she stayed in her room for a while before her mother forced her down to greet me, but after they became more comfortable they appeared to me as two joyful and entertaining children, so full of life, it was refreshing to see such innocence. Then when the oldest of them all came with his family, Cromwell that is, I discovered that, although he was a family man, he was also highly driven by work, in fact after we were introduced his first thought was to discuss his current position at his job with his father, while Penny sat with his mother and the twins played with Cory. And when the last, but not least, Creighton, arrived we all sat for dinner. Creighton himself seemed as driven by work, however there was a way he presented himself and how he communicated with his mother that gave the impression he was more motivated by family than work. Of course, they were so much more than the traits I described, but how can you fit an entire person into words. For the first time in a long while it felt as though someone cared for me. Oliver's mother asked me about how my mother was, and his father asked me about how I was doing at school, I don't think you notice how much you miss someone taking the time to talk to you, about you until you spend so long worrying about someone else. "Oliver told us you liked to write?" Creighton asked me, and although he did not sound judgemental the question made me nervous and I felt my hands beginning to sweat. "I do," I replied quickly, trying not to reveal the tremble in my voice. "Oliver likes to write poetry" Cromwell added, mocking Oliver a little, but not in a cruel way. "Oh enough" his mother said to them light-hearted as she knew they were only joking. I felt more confident knowing this family had very different opinions than mine, "I like to write horror stories," I said slowly filling with pride, "I love horror, you will have to let me read one, next time you're round" Oliver's father answered, I was in disbelief and so incredibly happy, although this was my best friend's father, he was giving me what I needed from my own. I felt I had an obligation to do as he bid and the next time, I saw him I did bring him a story.

The conversations for the rest of the night were endless. It was such a lively atmosphere and the only time I didn't mind being in a busy room. Laughter had danced around the us like it was a ballet performance, the smiles had acted like a light for the room. Even as dinner had ended and night was drawing closer, they did not let the energy die. After we had all eaten, we had gone to the sitting-room and the elders had a drink while we were given some juice. Although they drank, they did not become so intoxicated as to be unaware of what was happening in the room. At first, I was nervous to be around them as they drank for what I had seen of my father's drunk habits, but they did not change, they only became happier and more energetic. Oliver's father began to sing a song I don't remember much of it, but I do remember the lyrics.
No, nay, never
No, nay never no more
Will I play the wild rover?
No never, no more, the only reason I remember this part was because everyone in the room joined in at this point and when I heard it enough I, myself joined in too. I wasn't too sure what the song meant but although it had or seemed to have had sad lyrics, they sang it with such energy and made it sound so much happier than it was.

When the night was over, Oliver and Creighton had walked me home, which I highly appreciated because I wasn't confident walking alone in the dark and my

sense of direction was terrible. We laughed about some of the things that their mother and father had said which I cannot completely recollect now, and Creighton had asked us what we wanted to do when we left school. Oliver was not sure, but he was attracted to a career in law, which is a path I had also chosen as I wanted to please my father. At the time it seemed like my only option but as I have gotten older, I realised it wasn't and I regret, whole heartedly not taking the path that I knew I would have been more enthusiastic about sooner. "So, what do you boys want to do when you leave secondary school?" Creighton asked us, "I think I want to go into law." replied Oliver, "My father is a lawyer, I have always wanted to follow in his footsteps" Creighton laughed, "Why?" he asked me, "Because..." I couldn't answer, I only wanted to do law to make my father proud, but I was too embarrassed to admit that to them. "Ah don't worry about it I was only playing', I think if I did what my dad did, I would drive myself insane. But he would be proud. Did you tell him he was a builder?" Creighton looked over at Oliver, but Oliver was too busy kicking a stone to look back up at him. "No, I haven't I don't think. Did I Sam?"
"Look at this one." Creighton laughed and nudged Oliver hard, "He's always been the slowest out of all of us" he said while grabbing Oliver and pretending to box him, I laughed as well then replied to Oliver's question, "No you didn't. But what is wrong with being a builder?"

"Too much manual labour, I prefer sitting on my arse all day at my typewriter. I bet he didn't tell you what I did either?" I looked at Oliver guiltily but then replied regardless. "No, he didn't"

"I am a journalist for the paper. And a writer in my spare time."

"Not a good one," mocked Oliver and the two began to wrestle jokingly. When we arrived at my house Oliver

and Creighton looked at it in awe. "That's your house?" asked Oliver completely shocked. "Yes,"
"You weren't lying when you said your dad was a lawyer"
"Why would I lie," Creighton laughed as if I had missed the joke, "Anyway Oliver and I must be getting home before our mother calls out the town to search for us."
"Thank you for walking me home. I'll see you tomorrow at school Oliver!" I shouted as the two started to walk home, "See you tomorrow Sam!" I watched as Creighton grabbed Oliver into a headlock. An amusing sight that I envied. I wished I had an older brother, but instead I was the older brother of a younger sister. "Let go of me your big idiot" he said while Creighton walked with Oliver's head under his arm. He and Creighton left me at my house, walking home teasing each other further, I walked through my front door laughing.

I returned to an empty house. My imagination went wild as I went from room to room trying to find them. It wasn't until Claire had come in and explained it all. "Sam! You are back so late, your mum said you would have been home sooner than this." I panicked and felt my cheeks burn with shame, I felt as though I was being scolded. "It doesn't matter right now anyway. Your mum went into labour while you were away, so your dad had to come home early to take her to the hospital. They took Alex with them. I don't think they will let your mum out tonight so it will be just me and you." she said with a comforting smile, "is she okay?" I asked anxiously, "of course," I was not convinced but before I could say anything else she asked, "who was the older boy you were with?" she seemed a bit too interested which amused me, "It was Oliver's older brother Creighton, they walked me home."

"That was very nice of him, a true gentleman" she said as she glided through the sitting-room, blushing a little and then pulled a book out from the bookshelf and asked if I would like to sit and hear a story. She chose, to my displeasure, a Jane Austen novel, it was Northanger Abbey one that I did not waste my time reading after I had firmly decided that I did not like her novels. However, I did not have the heart or the energy, for that matter, to argue with her over her choice, so I sat obediently and listened to her. But eventually I did get bored of Jane Austen and to fix that I asked her if I could write her a story, "You want to write me a story? Well what kind of story?"
"A scary story."
"I have a better idea, why don't we both write each other a story, and then we'll show them to your mother and father, and they'll decide who is better?"
"That's a great idea. But not my father, just my mother," she looked at me confused but instead went along with it. She went next door and brought back with her two journals. "Here, I have used this one already, but this is a new one, you can keep it and write your stories in it." my eyes lit up at the journal that I now held in my hand, and where most would see just a journal I saw so many opportunities, the best thing about an imagination.

I don't think she liked my story very much. I wrote about a scientist who turned himself into an insect for a mad experiment, whereas she wrote a tragic love story much like those of Shakespeare. I didn't quite like hers either. But we did not just stop there, we continued to write stories, whether they were a page or twenty and we read them to each other. It was a wonderful night. At some point we must have fallen asleep because the next thing I remember is a loud knock at the door. I knew it wasn't my mother or my father, because why would they knock and after Claire had answered it was one female voice. It was gentle and soft but at the same time so different from my mother's, I tried to listen in as I pulled my weak body up right on the couch, but all I heard was mumbles and soon small footsteps, patting through the hall and up the stairs which I recognised as Alex. I followed her up the stairs and met her in her bedroom. She looked like a corpse, and I knew that at only ten years old she had, had the worst night of her life. She forced a small smile and then threw her weak and limp body onto her bed, I didn't see the point in asking her any questions, so I pulled off her shoes and tucked her in before I went back down to the sitting-room. I found Claire, sitting on the couch, rocking a new-born in her arms. I didn't need to ask to know that this was my newest sibling. She looked up, she smiled, but her eyes revealed that the smile was only a cover. She beckoned me over and introduced me, "Look Sam, it's your new baby sister, your mother and father named her Hanna. What do you think? Isn't she beautiful" she was beautiful, but I was lost in my thoughts and questions that my anxiety held me back from releasing? Instead of doing anything that would be appropriate to the situation I sat back on the couch and stared at the new-born that Claire continued to rock.

When we woke up the next morning, I could see Claire tried to make it seem as normal as possible, but as much as we appreciated her attempt she could not distract us from our mother and father being absent at such an inconvenient and strange time. Alex remained silent the entire morning during breakfast, and I followed her lead. It took Claire to break the silence with, "once your both done here we will go to the hospital to see your mother, I assume your father is there to, you'll have to miss school today Sam but don't worry I've called the head master." and that we did.

Claire called for a taxi and took us to the hospital.

CHAPTER THREE

My mother was in the same hospital as she worked, this gave me a strange sense of comfort as I knew she would be around people she knew and people who cared about her. Claire directed us to the reception then to the room, she waited outside as we went in, I had Hanna in my arms. She did not look like her, she looked like a human doll, only permitted to live when it interested others. She did not move, in fact I think she was asleep, but when she heard us move closer she twitched her head a little to try and face us, it was clear, however, she was too weak to move, she opened her mouth a little to try and speak but instead all that came out was a squeak. She cried a little which scared Alex and when Alex began to cry, Hanna had awoke and screamed her lungs out, I took them both out and handed Hanna to Claire, she was in tears as well which I was shocked to see, as she did not fully know my mother, she was only acquainted with her when she was appointed as our nanny over the summer holidays. Seeing them cry made me feel so far away from them, and at the same time I felt resentment towards them for being so weak emotionally. I felt they were responsible for their own vulnerability.

I went back into the room where my mother lay and I

held her hand, she was still in tears. My heart broke and I felt a deep pain in between my ribs, a pain that brought the feeling of dread that I could never escape. I was now in the same position as those who waited for me outside, and just as I resented them, I began to resent myself. I hugged her tight, I was naively hoping that hugging her as tight as I was would keep her soul in her body so she could live. She whispered to me, "Look after them, they will need you more than they will need your father, I'm so sorry Sammy, I love you all", I don't believe she meant to whisper but she was just so weak. She clutched me with the remaining of her strength and as she slipped from my grasp, I knew she had left us. I called for a nurse in panic, even though I knew there was nothing they could do. They went in, Claire stood with us outside, as we all drowned in tears. They came out and broke the news that she was gone. I don't feel as though I actually heard them, the information didn't seem to stick, I felt nothing. Alex seemed to have taken all the grief from me and Hanna. We left the hospital and then it clicked that my father wasn't there, or outside. I asked Claire about it, but she pretended that she didn't hear me and instead dried her eyes and then Alex's and called for another taxicab.

Claire took us home and Alex went straight to bed, we didn't see her or our father for the rest of the week but at least we knew where Alex was. Claire, out of no obligation, took it upon herself to become our carer for the time that our father was gone. She and her widowed mother helped transform the nursery into a bedroom for Hanna as my mother became too sick to do so herself and my father worked so often it left no time for them to be prepared for their third child. Claire and her mother had looked around the town for cheap cots and furniture for the baby, and her mother had pulled together enough money to keep us all fed and comfortable. I pushed myself to continue to go to school. Oliver caught on to my mood and pressed me to tell him what was causing me to be so lethargic. I told him. It felt like a relief to open up about my father's absence and my mother's death, emotions I had no idea I had started to bubble up to the surface. I cried so hard and was humiliated at my lack of self-control. But he appeared to be understanding and sympathetic to my situation, he told me that he would be happy to help in any way he could and offered me to join him and his family once again for dinner, I felt obligated to decline however, because although Claire was there with Alex, I could not abandon her like my father did and my mother told me to look after both her and Hanna. So when I explained my situation to him the next again day he told me his mother had extended the invitation to both Alex and Hanna, I was overwhelmed with the kindness that I received from the McCarthy's, and I told him that I would discuss it with Alex and Claire before making any decisions.

As the weekend approached, however I completely forgot to tell Alex and Claire about the McCarthy's proposal, and it was soon too late as we had an unexpected visit from our father, one that Claire did not seem to be pleased with and as I have grown, I now realise it was because he appeared to have been drinking the days away since our mother died. He struggled up to the top step which alerted us all and Claire and I had gone to the hallway to see what the noises were. When he stumbled through the doorway, he brought with him a foul smell and looked like he had just come from a sewer, he looked Claire dead in the eyes with unjustifiable rage which I could see made her uncomfortable, but as bold as she was, she did not show him any weakness. He then darted his eyes to me as I stood dumbstruck next to her, his eyes filled with more rage. "Where are your sisters?" he slurred in an angry tone, "Alex is in the sitting-room with Hanna" he then looked back at Claire, "get them ready for their mother's funeral. You will be paid in full of extra for your time" he didn't ask Claire, he demanded and although he said he would pay her, he did not respect her. Claire did as she was told and got Alex and Hanna dressed in their best clothes, I got myself ready and met them in the hall. My father soon stumbled into the hall to, he had showered and changed his clothes, but he still looked half dead, and his breath alone could intoxicate anyone near it. He pulled out a flask that was in his pocket and took a large gulp from it, then he proceeded to his car. When Claire saw that he intended to drive us to the funeral she offered to pay for the taxi. My father took this as an insult but agreed out of spite. He demanded she accompanied us, because he was not planning on coming home for that night and would need her to take care of us. Claire was kind enough to agree and I had to stop myself from releasing a sigh of release.

My mother's funeral was the first one I had been to, but it would certainly not be the last. Although on the way to England many died on the ship, they were not given a funeral like this. A lot of my mother's fellow nurses attended, as well as Ms Maxwell, who I was shocked to see but I soon realised she was just there for my father which was just another thing he added on to the ever growing list of disappointments he had given me. Alex seemed lifeless at the funeral, she stood still and stared at the coffin the entire time, Claire stood close beside Alex holding her hand while also holding the baby. For a moment I got lost looking at her, *how can anyone as young as this woman, want to look after three children, that was of no relation to her?* I wish at this time, I could have thanked Claire for everything she did for us, but I was too young to consider the lengths she went to as something unnecessary on her part. We did not see my father for a week or two afterwards, I lost track of the time through the chaos that followed the funeral. As of this time I did not go to stay with the McCarthy's, but I did go to dinner at their house every Sunday, they were the highlight of my life at this time. They became the only real family I had. I kept my situation as hidden as I could from them however, they were already doing so much, and I did not want to worry them further. It was a Sunday I came home from the McCarthy's that I found my father sitting on his own and Claire was gone, he told me he was back, and we would not be seeing Claire ever again or so was his thoughts at this time. My heart broke and I realized how much I wanted him to leave again so we could stay with Claire.

Three years had passed Hanna got older, and Alex reached the age to go to secondary school, things changed drastically. We discovered that due to Alex abandoning her studies so she could take care of our mother and then Hanna, she would not be allowed to attend secondary school for she was so far behind. Claire had become an apprentice nurse at the Lewes Victoria Hospital, and she had never seemed prouder in the time that we had known her. On top of this our father felt more obliged to stay intoxicated to get through a day at work. He didn't let Claire know, or anyone for that matter that we would need to be looked after for the time that he was working. So, while I was at school, Alex was left at home alone with Hanna. One night when I came home from school I found him sitting alone in the dark in the sitting room, and as I walked past trying to avoid him the best I could, he called me over to his presence, his voice shot shivers straight through me like a bullet for it was so empty. I tiptoed over, holding my breath, to where he was sitting,

he demanded me to sit on the chair across from his, and as I sat down, he began to interrogate me about school. "How are you getting on?" he asked as he circled his glass with his thumb, "Fine" I said cautiously in return, his eyes darted to me but he did not move his head, "Just fine?" he asked coldly, I could feel my heart beating strong and fast under the pressure, "It's good" I corrected and then I took the opportunity to tell him about Oliver and our shared passion for literature, this did not please him, he straightened up sharply and replied to my enthusiasm with conviction. "This Oliver, is it a boy or a girl?" I could tell he was teasing about the passion we shared, he never did find it "manly", but I replied anyway, "he is a boy" I said quietly, remaining cautious "And are you a boy or a girl?"
"A boy"
"Are you sure?"
"yes"
"Louder!"
"YES!"
"Then bloody act like one..." he seemed hesitant at the end of his sentence, like he was going to continue to say something else but did not know how. "Go to your room, I will call you for dinner in an hour". He did in fact remember to call us for dinner on this night, however it was not his dinner, he asked Claire over to cook for us and then he left. I do not believe he consulted her in the decision, prior.

Claire had made a beautiful dinner, we had a stew that she had originally made for her and her mother and had some left over, then after dinner we did our usual, play games and when it was closer to curfew, we told stories. I do not believe I was supposed to witness what came next, but I did, and I feel as though it is important to include into my story. I had awoken late that night to use the restroom, I heard Claire speak to another woman who I assumed was her mother as she had an older voice, but they spoke like old friends. When I had went down to the sitting-room in the morning to find my assumption was correct. The part of the conversation I caught, gave me a slight bit of hope, and urge to beg Claire to take us away but something held me back. I heard Claire say "It's ridiculous the way he acts. When I came in today, he reeked of alcohol, it's like he has no care for his own children and now he is away again. And the whole town knows where he is", I could tell she was trying to keep her voice down, but it did not work, I heard everything from the top of the stairs, my usual eavesdropping position. She continued, "I was here for those children, day and night, I don't understand why we can't just take them in ourselves? It's not like he would bother, he doesn't bother with them while they are here"

"Claire you know why we can't take them in, they are not our children and although your heart is there, no one will allow an unrelated woman or man, to take someone else's children, no matter how many claims you throw into the fire that show how unfit that man is. There is no evidence that the children have been mistreated, therefore it will be a useless attempt and could harm your reputation." the older woman's voice said, my heart sunk to hear the logic but I, as a naïve child, held up the hope that Claire would take us away. When my father returned the next morning I watched Claire's actions eagerly, hoping she would stand up to him so we could go away with her and live better lives, however she obeyed the older woman's voice and went back to her own house after giving us a warm goodbye. We all lived in fear of the demon that possessed my father, but as time went on, I was getting closer and closer to going to university, and leaving the hell that was created, by poor sisters however were not as lucky as I with this opportunity.

Oliver and I had done everything together at this point, we studied together, we joined clubs together, and when the opportunity to choose our own classes had occurred, we each picked the same. Although we both had an intense passion for English, we had the realistic expectations of finding a career in that path, therefore we both chose to pursue law. In our second last year of secondary school, we built a suitable experience that would allow us to secure a place into a suitable law degree. Of course, we applied for the same universities, but we never fully thought it through if we both got a place into different universities but thankfully it did not come to that as you will soon find out. The thought of leaving for university in a year, from this point in time, gave me anxiety. I was afraid to leave my sisters alone with the demon in our home. Not that I was any form of protector to them while I was present, but at least I would be able to, prevent them from experiencing any extreme acts of violence that could affect them throughout the rest of their lives if that event ever occurred. Or at least that is what I told myself at this point.

There was a time I came home from an after-school debate club on a Thursday night, it would only be a year before I would leave for a University in London. I found my sisters in the sitting room, with faces of stone that were filled with fear that they were trying not show. My father was not present at this point, but I could tell he was not long gone and would not be long returning. When Alex saw me, she cried, and Hanna imitated when she saw her sister's tears. She ran to me and hugged me, I tried to ask what was going on, but the words hid in my throat like a subconscious being was telling me I did not want to know. A few moments later, my father had returned with a bottle in his hand. He looked at me and pointed to the couch where Hanna was sitting, both me and Alex took our seats. What came next, I will never be able to erase from my mind.

CHAPTER FOUR

He began to talk about my mother and her pregnancy, "I knew it was a bad idea," he began, "I felt it in my bones how it was going to destroy her, I will admit I didn't know how, but I knew."
"Dad, please-"
"Enough Aleksandria!" he cut her off sharply and I believe at this point Alex and I both knew where this was going, and Alex subtly put her arm around Hanna without breaking eye contact with the demon in front of us. He then went on to the day she gave birth which was believed to be the cause of her death. At this point in history we did not have the medical advancement that you, who may be reading this do, at your point in history. "I got the message from my boss that my wife needed me. It was humiliating. The way all those other men looked at me with pity, how dare they! But nonetheless I had to leave, and my boss was more than happy to allow me. I rushed home trying to maintain my patience and my anger because I didn't want anything to happen to her. She was the love of my life, the one I was supposed to be with." he looked away from us in shame at the tears that were running down his cheeks, "when I got home I made my way to the bedroom, I knew she was there not because it was where she was for the majority of the pregnancy but

because of the screaming. I'm sure you will remember what was happening Aleksandria? It was killing your mother." she shot a deadly look at Hanna, "when I got to the room nothing would have prepared me for what I saw. She looked like a corpse, she was so pale, her eyes were so empty. The girl next door kept patting her head with a cold cloth because Nadia was drenched in sweat. "what happened?" I asked the girl, Aleksandria seemed so frightened but I couldn't console you while Nadia was in so much danger. "She seems to have gone in to labour, but she's losing so much blood, it doesn't make much sense! She needs to go to the hospital," the girl told me all in one breath, I was impressed. I had not a moment to think. I picked Nadia up and hailed down the first taxicab I saw, I wouldn't have been able to keep Nadia safe while I was driving. I demanded the driver to not ask questions and just go, but he was looking between Aleksandria, who was crying her lungs out and myself, so I pulled her into the cab aside us." it no longer seemed he was talking to us, but to himself, nonetheless we sat still and quiet allowing him to finish in hopes he would release the demons that held him to this misery. "When we got to the hospital, I saw many of the nurses that worked with her, Aleksandria was still crying. Thankfully all the nurses recognized Nadia and one took the child away while the other led me to a bed where I was to lay my sweetheart. "Sir, you shouldn't be here right now, you will only get into the doctor's way," one of the nurses told me, but I refused to allow anyone to separate me from my wife, "I will not leave her." I said as I was clutching on to her hand as if somehow it would keep her soul in her body. She had lost consciousness in the cab, but I made sure she was still breathing. "sir please!" before I could snap at the impertinent nurse the doctor came. "Let him be here for his wife," he gestured for me to sit back down. "Mr Nowak can you tell me what happened?"

"My neighbour said she went into labour, but she was bleeding too heavy. I was at work. I didn't know this would happen,"

"Please sir, it is okay, these things happen" the doctor had assured me, but I couldn't tear myself away from the guilt." now our father was completely sobbing, he stood up and poured a glass of whisky and brought both the bottle and glass back with him to the chair, where he continued the tale, "the doctor had listened to her chest and her stomach, he nodded to a nurse and he then he addressed me once again, "Mr Nowak, your wife cannot give birth naturally, so we will have to take her to operating room"

"Absolutely not! Wake her up and she will have a natural birth, or kill the thing if you must!" he looked at me as if I were a mad man, I realised I had to correct my statement before he had me locked away in a mad house. "Please doctor, I cannot lose my wife, I cannot live without her, we already have two children," he grabbed my shoulder as if it would provide some form of comfort and they wheeled Nadia away from me. I paced for the entire time she was in that room until I was finally greeted by one of the nurses who assisted the doctor during the operation, "Mr Nowak?" I could only nod, "The doctor has finished the caesarean section and you have a beautiful baby girl," her smile dropped. "Unfortunately, due to many complications, your wife will not survive the week, I am so sorry." I felt like I was being paralyzed as I sat listening to the evil this nurse had spoken, "You can see her if you like?"

"I will not look at the monster that has just killed my wife," she looked at me stunned but then continued. "The baby and your wife are in the same room." I begged her then to show me. When I entered that room, I could feel my heart ache as I looked upon the corpse of Nadia, the one who made each day seem bright when we were still in our youth. It then hit me. Everything I did to disrespect her, I had no right, and it was not too late to take it all back." he took a deep breath which looked painful and then tried to continue, "I sat down next to her, and she opened her eyes, they were completely lifeless and empty, her skin was so pale it was grey and when she reached for my hand, her own shivered hard with how weak she had become. "Bart," she began, "look at the baby, she's beautiful, she looks like me" I took one quick glance, but I couldn't bear to look a second longer. To sooth my wife I agreed, "You will look after them all, Bart? Please?" her voice was so soft and weak, as she spoke it seemed like she was putting all her energy in each individual word. "Of course! They are my children as well"

"But I know you're always working and that you pride yourself on putting that first before anything-"

"That will change Nadia. Please stay with us to see how I will change." I saw her eyes fill with tears and I was introduced to the pain she felt that I could not bear to accept. "You know I can't stay any longer, dear, but it's okay, I will be in heaven with my mother and father, and your mother and father, we will all keep you safe from there."

"Don't talk nonsense Nadia, you have to stay here, now isn't your time to go yet." she always had this look that told me I was being a fool without her making a sound, and she gave me that look now. "I give you my blessing, Bart, to be with Abigail after I'm gone, but only if she is good to my children. And I forgive you, for betraying my trust to be with her." she said this so calmly, so matter-of-fact but I could not bear being discovered, I stood up, "How did you know about that?"

"Bart, dear, a woman can always tell when she has lost the ability to keep her husband's interest."

"But Nadia, you know I always have loved you the most, and I always will, there will never be a woman who can replace you in my life, or in our children's life, you are-"

"Bart, I will hear no more, bring the children to me tomorrow so I can say farewell to all of you. And take the children to America please." at this point I could hear no more, so I left the room and found the nurse who was watching over Aleksandria, and I gave her money to take her home. I left the hospital and I do not remember a second since." his eyes darted to Hanna with such fury it made me sick with nerves, "All of this would have never have happened, if a monster did not tear its way through my wife." he began to sob once more and this, for some reason caused me great fear, I had never seen my father cry. And now with all his temper I can only imagine how he was feeling. He had the idea that men do not cry, and for him to be crying in front of his children... I braced myself for his next action. He darted up like a bullet from a gun. He grabbed Hanna from my sister's arms, and began to beat her to the ground, with nothing but his fists, but his fists must have felt like mallets to poor Hanna.

Alex shook out her shock then darted up herself and screamed, she tried to pull Hanna from the ground and away from the crossfire. But that only got her beaten herself. I sat... I sat on the couch, with my eyes to the ground and I began to cry. The shame I feel for this moment will never leave me; I have been haunted with it ever since. To my sisters, Alex Melvin, and Hanna Nowak, I am so sorry, I was not deserving of the kindness you gave me even after this moment. This was the night my father disappeared for a very long period, Alex and I took Hanna to the hospital. We called a taxi to get there, we did not want to worry Claire. When asked how Hanna ended up in this state, we both agreed on the story that she was attacked by a group of older boys while we were on our way home from after school clubs. Hanna had a broken arm and fractured ribs; her eye was swollen out of its socket. Alex had less severe injuries. No broken bones but she did have a fractured wrist and her eye was also rather swollen. I don't think they fully believed us because I was the only one who remained un-scathed by the supposed attack, but they didn't seem to care enough to get the real story.

"What do we do Sam?" Alex whispered to me in the corridor while Hanna was having her injuries tended to, "Should we go to Claire?"
"No! No one needs to know what he did." I snapped at her. She looked up to me with tears flooding to her eyes, but I did not back down, "But what about Hanna?"
"Alex, he is still our dad, so what if he made one mistake he is grieving. He loves us, he's just struggling a little." Alex went quiet after this and dropped the subject. After Hanna's check-up our plan was to get home on our own but to our surprise we were to be picked up by a woman. The nurse came to us and said, "Your babysitter has come to pick you up, she is just in the hall." our thoughts were that it would be Claire, but we were crushed to see Ms Maxwell had returned.
"Such smart children aren't they" she said to the nurse, "wise, way beyond their years" replied the nurse with a suspicious tone as if she knew Ms Maxwell was hiding something. She held Hanna's hand like a responsible caretaker and walked us outside. "It was smart of you all to keep quiet about your dad's... accident. You don't want him to go to prison now do you?"
"Of course, not Ms Maxwell," I replied because I knew Alex did not care at this moment and would not think twice about telling Ms Maxwell exactly how she felt. When we returned home, we found our dad sitting in his usual spot, drunker than he was when we left for the

hospital. "Bart, I brought the children home, you will never believe what happened, the girls were attacked on their way home." he stumbled into the hallway almost giddy, "Oh no my poor girls. And let me guess you just stood back and allowed it to happen you pathetic excuse for a man." he slurred, I was convinced he didn't remember what he did because he was that drunk, "You will remember Abigail won't you, Alexandria and Samuel? Hanna won't because she is far too young but basically, she is your new step-mum" he laughed repulsively and then kissed her, to intimately for our young eyes. "She's not our mum" Alex snapped, I looked at her in shock and started to fear for her. Instead of saying anything Bart just stared at her with anger in every part of his expression, but just like a switch he snapped back to normal, "Now you lot go play me and your mum have some business to discuss regarding these boys who has attacked you girls." he slurred again and shot me a deadly look, "Samuel why don't you go out and find where you left your backbone and then come back in when your man enough to protect your sisters, hmm?"

"But it's raining?" his eyes raged at me, his face went red and I could feel my panic build up inside of me in seconds, I knew I crossed a line. He grabbed me by my collar and then dragged me outside, I can remember Hanna screaming, and Alex trying to calm her down while Ms Maxwell, or 'Abigail' screamed at her to shut up. I was too afraid to breathe. He threw me outside in every literal sense of the word and locked the door, and there I was to sit until 'I became a man'.

In the following year Alex decided that the best way for her and Hanna to continue to survive would be if she found herself a job and moved out with Hanna, since things didn't seem to be getting better and our father's temper only increased as he sunk into his alcoholism.

She was old enough for a job as a housemaid or in the local shop, she had turned sixteen that year. But regardless of her being old enough for a job she was too young to take on this responsibility of maintaining a household and caring for a child. It should have been me who took them both away from that hell, I failed them and my mother by neglecting my responsibility as their brother and a man, it was my job to take care of them and protect them from harm but I simply couldn't. It didn't take her long to secure a position in the pub in town, the owners wife took a shine to her and her dedication, and as she worked there the owners wife became a role model for her, I believe her name was Elizabeth but she preferred Liz. Once her first wage came in, she and Liz went looking for affordable flats that would be big enough for both her and Hanna. My innocent sister had gone as far as offering to host me in her new flat when she found one until I had finished school, but I refused. I refused both out of having too much pride and guilt. I only had a few months left before I went to a university in London with Oliver and I felt that I could handle whatever came from it in that time. I avoided talking about my home life with Oliver although he did make it clear that if I ever needed help, he would be the first to provide whatever help I needed. I refused out of pride and the feeling that I deserved to be miserable after what I allowed to happen to my sisters. I remained at my dad's home with Ms Maxwell as his new 'whore'. I was still at school and did not see the use of taking time away from my studies when I was already so near getting the qualifications I needed for a degree in law. Oliver had somehow guessed what was happening and he went to every extent to pull me from it, and he always asked how Alex was getting on. But I could never answer him truthfully as we became distant after she left. Every time I tried to talk to my father we were interrupted by Ms Maxwell. I continued writing my stories to get through the day but of course it was always in private. I wrote mainly monster stories back then, about vampires, witches and the undead. I consumed, solely, novels that had those themes, so I had constant inspiration. I liked scary stories more than anything else. I once wrote a ghost story about a woman and her child that moved into an estate quite like ours but were haunted by the ghost the estates past mistresses. And when the woman with her child introduced a man to the estate, strange things happened. They would find their lights flashing, the stoves turned on without them doing so themselves and it was turned up to the maximum heat. This was my only escape from the reality that was Ms Maxwell and my broken father. My imagination became a weapon against the outside world, and I could spend hours in my head making up horror stories whenever I pleased. I would become a regular at the McCarthy's on Sunday's for Mrs McCarthy's delicious dinners. Creighton would sometimes joke that I was one of the family, which was an idea that brought me great joy. When I became comfortably acquainted with the entire family, I would talk to Creighton a lot about his career and how he got involved with it, I don't think he was used to being asked personal questions. However, the main topic of conversation around the dinner table was Oliver and I going to university to study law. His family was so proud of him as they all knew there was a lot of money in law, but they weren't looking to scrounge off him they only wanted him to have the life they dreamt of for their children.

When I was at home I could see my dad's sadness, I could feel his grief and I knew if I could get through to him and make him see that he was not going the right way and my mother would be looking down on him in shame, he would change. But Ms Maxwell needed him

broken, because when he was broken, she was rich. I waited for a day that I knew Ms Maxwell would be out to try and save my father. It was a Saturday, "Dad, are you awake?" I asked as he lay with his head low on his armchair. "Are you hungry? I can make you something to eat if you like?" he looked up at me stiffly, but he struggled to move his limp and poisoned body on his own so I had to help him up and through to the kitchen where he slumped on the chair. "How about some bacon and eggs?" I asked but he did not answer, I knew he liked bacon and eggs because my mother made it for him every morning, he didn't have work, so I made it for him anyway. As I sat the plate down in front of him with a knife and fork, he dug in immediately. I sat with him, but I did not eat, "dad?" he looked up at me to show me he was listening, "do you ever think of mum?" I said so quietly, I was shocked he heard me, I was shocked I had the nerves to ask him, "Of course I do," he replied defensively, "do you believe in heaven?" I asked, "I did for a while after your mother was here, but I don't know if I can anymore" his voice quivered and I thought he would start crying again, "Are you okay dad?" before he could answer the dreaded Ms Maxwell had come in with shopping bags filled with new clothes. "I told you not to bother your father while he wasn't feeling himself." she demanded, "he was hungry, and we were just having a conversation!"
"Don't raise your voice at me!"
"Don't be so unreasonably wicked and I won't feel the need to in the first place!"
"Bart are you going to let him talk to me like that?"
"That's enough Samuel"
"Dad can't you see she is using you!?" he stood up in rage and slammed his fist against the table, "That's enough! Get out of my house!" I didn't argue, I didn't whimper, I did what I was told.

For my last month of school, I took up the offer that the McCarthy's gave me to stay at their house until both Oliver and I were ready to go to university. Nearing our final exams, we got the news that we were both accepted into the University of Cambridge which was situated in London. Both
Oliver's mother and father were so proud of us. To this day I have never forgotten the kindness and acceptance I received from the McCarthy's. They are the most wonderful people I have ever met, and anyone acquainted with them should feel lucky.

CHAPTER FIVE

When the time had come for Oliver and me to leave for university, I had practically moved in with the McCarthy's. Oliver's mum had treated me like another one of her sons and I began to bond with his younger brother and sister and treated them like my own siblings. Which meant that when the time came for us to move to London to study law it was difficult for all parties involved. The year was 1904, the day before we left, I thought it was time I saw my sisters again after months of neither of us making the effort to contact one another. I had not visited them since Alex had moved out with Hanna and I helped them move, of course our dad wouldn't bother, and Ms Maxwell had convinced him that Alex leaving was disrespectful and a betrayal. I felt guilty about waiting so long to see them, the guilt buried into my chest so deep that I almost didn't go. But I could not leave without checking they were doing well.

I gave no warning prior to my arrival so I can't blame Alex for her shock and confusion as she opened the door. "Sam! Is there something wrong? Where's dad?" "I won't lie I have no idea where dad is, but if he is home then I shall see him next after I speak to Claire," she waited a moment and then continued, "what do you want?" she sounded uncomfortable, as if it were a stranger in front of her and not her brother, "I was hoping we could sit, I haven't seen Hanna or you in while. I don't think we've spoken since before you moved out" she appeared as though she was being cautious of me, "I was just about to go to work, but I have some time for a tea." she permitted me entrance. Her flat was typical for a woman her age with her wage, she kept it clean as you would expect, in fact the only thing that made it obvious that it was home to a low income woman and a young child, was the size and the toys on the floor. "What a lovely flat" I praised, Alex did not seem too amused with my remark, she stood next to the kettle with her back to me, Hanna had come running into the living room with excitement as she found out I was in. "Look how big you're getting" I said as I embraced her. She may have been growing tall, but she was also growing thin, they both were. This was when my guilt fully sunk in. "Are you both eating well?" I asked trying not to impose, "We're fine" she replied flatly.

She brought over two cups of tea for us and a small glass of milk for Hanna, she directed Hanna back to the room to play. "who will be looking after Hanna while you're at work?"
"The woman next door usually does it" she said bluntly, "she's a nice woman, Hanna seems to like her, every time I come home she tells me such strange stories of how they played explorers or vampires or whatever nonsense I'm sure Hanna had forced upon the poor woman. But she does not complain, and the best part is she does it for free, all she asks is that whenever she needs some help to tidy her home that I clean for her."
"Sounds like a good deal" I replied trying to bring a lighter tone to the conversation, this was not successful. She glared at me before she spoke the words, "what are

you doing here?"

"I'm going to university tomorrow in London, with Oliver. I will be studying law"

"Right, so why bother coming here?"

"I did not feel right leaving without saying goodbye"

"I didn't even know you were still around in the first place" I laughed a little, but I knew she meant what she said with such resentment. I changed the subject to Hanna, "how is Hanna doing? She seems happy here, has she started school?"

"She is doing fine, Sam." she snapped but then continued on in a more delicate tone, "but I do not have time to take her to school and go to work at the same time, not to mention the cost. And anyway, I think she may be a bit slower than the other children, after what happened to her."

"What makes you think that?"

"I have found her sitting in the middle of the floor staring into nothing, she stutters sometimes and the woman next door has told me about how she will burst into tears for no reason, I asked her to keep it to herself and she has gave me that respect. I ask you to keep it to yourself to, she may be slow, but she will be worth something one day. If anyone found out, you know what they will do with her."

"Is there anything I can do?"

"What makes you so interested in us now? You can't do anything anyway you're off to London tomorrow, and what would you do? You can't fix this by sitting silent Sam"

"I'm so sorry Alex, I-"

"Enough," she snapped again and then she became highly emotional, "I do not want to hear one more word, you are my older brother, you should be the one working and looking after me and Hanna, I should not be alone! But that's what you gave me, and for that I wish nothing to do with you" I could see her holding back tears that I caused. "Alex please" I begged "LEAVE! Samuel, Hanna and I have been fine without you and dad, we certainly don't need you coming in here and ruining it." I left. Only a weak man leaves his family to rot in a hole alone, a strong man would do everything I haven't, but it's now too late to change it.

I went to my father's home after attempting to speak with Claire who I learned had moved in with her new husband after the death of her mother. I found my father in a terrible state. The house was dark and cold. The dishes that I left behind were still at the sink with new life growing on top of it. The house smelled of death even though no death had occurred inside of it. I found my father sitting among a heap of glass bottles, some smashed, some not, some half empty, some empty entirely. It was our sitting-room, but now this was not, nor was it our house. This was the hell of a man who buried himself so far into his own grave he couldn't climb back out. I felt a strong hit of emotion meet me at this sight. I felt tears rising in my eyes, but I hid them in case he noticed. I walked towards the body on the armchair, slowly like I was a child again trying to sneak a book from the bookshelf while Ms Maxwell was asleep. When I got near enough, I cautiously said out loud, "dad?" there was no response, I walked round to the front of the armchair and found him lying lifeless with his eyes open and filled with his own tears. It seemed like he was struggling to breathe. Like every breath was a knife that dug into his chest further than it already had been since my mother had passed. "Oh, dad" I said with shock but careful with my volume as I didn't want to startle him for various reasons. I tried to pull him up so he could sit up straight, I thought it may have helped his breathing. He acted like a stubborn child and made a weird groan, this broke me, for it showed the man who portrayed himself as unbreakable to his children was now too weak to say a single word. I knelt in front of him instead and hugged him. He hugged me back and we both sat there in tears. I was still nervous; however, I feared the demon that possessed him was still remaining within this image of a man who was once my father.

After a very long few minutes he pushed me away violently. I could feel my cheeks burn with both shame and fear but before I could react, he laughed and said, "Weakling, what will you ever become? I put so much effort into making you a man and instead you stand in front of me a pansy," he chuckled "you aren't even standing!" he laughed demonically, and I used my rage at this moment to stand once again. "You will become nothing! You're nor man or boy, even a boy can stand up for himself when he needs to, all you do is quiver! You are nothing! Your mother will be looking down on you in shame for what her only son has become!" I could not hold back my rage after he finished his sentence, "at least I was strong enough to stand by my family when they needed me, I may not be able to stand up to you but that is because you are nor man or boy! You're not even human! You are a monster. If my mother will be disappointed in anyone it will be you, the man she put her trust in to look after her children! If she knew that she was putting her faith in a demon and not a man, maybe she would have married someone else in the first place! If she knew about your betrayal when she was alive, she would have died from the heartache, that you would have caused. If god knew what you truly were, he would have taken you out of this world and not her!" I stormed out of the house, I heard Bart slump back into his chair and weep hard. This was the last time I spoke to my father until he was on his own deathbed.

I returned to the McCarthy's immediately after, as I didn't have an ounce of energy left to go for a walk or to the pub. They asked where I had been since I looked like I had just been to war, I told them that I appreciated the concern they had but I was too exhausted to explain or think about the day's events, they understood, and allowed me to retire to bed early. I had just lost both my parents, my sister wanted nothing more to do with me for reasons that I could only blame myself for. I was alone in my own mind. The kindness of the McCarthy's was not enough to conquer the pain that the day had caused.

The morning after I woke up early and felt a lot better than I did the night before. I was packed and ready to leave for the train station hours before it was time to, which was a good thing since it took Oliver a long time to pack himself. It took all four of us to get through half of the things he wanted to take. I think at the time he may have thought he was moving out for good. Eventually we had to involve the youngers to help him pack as well. That was comical. They were constantly teasing him on how much he wanted to take and about all his "sentimental". "What's this?" asked Nolan, holding up a ragged teddy bear that looked like it had lost all of its stuffing and then was thrown around a muddy field, Oliver snatched it out of her hand, "It's a bear gran and grandad gave to me when I was born, it's sentimental,"
"Oliver if I hear that word one more time, I will crack," interrupted Mr McCarthy, I stood in the doorway chuckling, "what are you laughing at?" he asked defensively, "you'll regret only bringing that box,"
"It's not permanent, and I don't think you'll have enough space for a third of all this stuff," I replied, "I'll make space," he demanded and then snatched the teddy bear back out of Nolan's hand. "do you not think you've

gone a bit overboard with all of this stuff son? Me and your mum would keep this stuff for you in your room anyway when you come back, and if you wanted any of it while you're away we'll bring it through to you when we come and visit." Oliver's dad thankfully convinced him, and the packing was a lot easier and efficient. It was a family dynamic I craved and all though it was right in front of me I felt so far away from it all. When it was finally time to leave tears were shed by the McCarthy's. Oliver's mother was the worst, I was almost relieved that there was no room in the car for her to come with us as well all the way to the train station. Oliver hugged his younger two siblings and hugged his mother an excessive amount of time before he finally left. On the way Oliver's father had asked me "is there anything you need to get from your old house Sam? We can go right now if needs be, we have plenty of time" "No thank you, there's nothing there anymore."

CHAPTER SIX

The university building was stunning to say the least. It was constructed of a handsome gothic architecture which made it look like an old castle from a horror story. The courtyard was its best feature in my opinion. It was surrounded by naturally grown flowers and plants. For the time of year, they were so vibrant, I should mention it was the beginning of September and we were reaching autumn so for the flowers to look like they were in the prime of spring was strange, yet magical. When we were given our assigned dormitory rooms, we were relieved to discover our request to be in the same hall was heard and after we un-packed we went exploring the local town. It was surprising to see how many cafes and pubs there were surrounding our university. It was perfect for those who enjoyed social activities and showed how welcome the town was to newcomers, which would only make sense since it was the home of such a large university. After walking for perhaps thirty minutes we found a small cafe with very few customers. At first we were unsure whether or not to enter as it seemed the place that only locals dined in and we would not be welcome, but we were too tired to make our way back to the university without first taking a break, so we took the risk. To our delightful surprise everyone was welcoming. An older man was sitting at a table on his own was facing the staff and it seemed they were enjoying a friendly conversation, however when we came in he greeted us as if we were his old friends, "I was wondering if you two were coming in," he laughed and after looking at each other we joined in nervously, "don't mind him" added one of the cooks, I noticed he had a Prussian accent, but I didn't bother to question him about it in fear of offending him. "you from the university?" the man asked, "just moved into the halls today," Oliver replied with such confidence, "not many of the students come here, I'm Brinley," responded the old man and he held out his hand but did not stand up. We both went forward to shake his hand, the cook joined in once again, "he scares them all away," we all laughed, it was a great comfort to see how comfortable they were with each other. Oliver and I took a seat next to the window, "I'll get the waitress," the cook told us as we sat down, and he disappeared back into the kitchen.

Soon after we were greeted by the most beautiful woman I had ever seen in my life, "hi, I'm Claudia, what can I get for you both?" I couldn't speak, I was in too much awe and felt far too nervous to make so much as a sound, "hi Claudia, I'm Oliver and that fool over there is Sam," I realised at this moment I was staring, I shook myself out of my haze and greeted her, "hi" was all I could say, "I'll have a coffee and... the soup of the day" Oliver said, Claudia had written the order down then looked at me, "and you?"
"just the same," I responded awkwardly, she just nodded and smiled, "okay, I'll bring it over when it's ready," then she walked away. Oliver laughed quietly, "what's funny?" I asked, wondering if I missed something, "you" he replied laughing harder, "what do you mean?"
"You were so awkward, the poor lassie will be too

scared to come back to our table,"
"Was I really that bad?"
"Worse,"
"Oh no"
"Don't worry about it, it was more funny than scary," assured Oliver, but I was too far into my anxiety to believe him. I was only released of my concerns when Claudia returned to our table with our order and this time, I tried to not be so awkward.

We ended up staying at the cafe for a good few hour and had a lot of coffee which kept us up for most of the night. Needless to say, our first day, which was filled with lectures due to it being an induction day for first years, was hard to say the least since we found ourselves running strictly on sleep deprivation. After the induction took place there was a fair with the purpose to introduce us to all the different clubs and activities the university provided. Oliver was immediately attracted to the universities football team and jumped at the chance to try out for it. I, on the other hand did not find any activities which took my interest. There was of course the football team which I would never have considered, there was a debate club which you would think I would have been interested in, but there was far too many others signing up and I wouldn't have had the confidence to debate with such an audience. But there was one treasure hidden away with no one signing up. I approached the booth with excitement but also apprehension, I asked the man what his activity was, and he looked at me with slight confusion, as if he wasn't sure I was real or a delusion. "It's a writer's group," he responded ardently, I felt my heart jump and I thought that this was a sign. I ran to Oliver and dragged him to the stall and we both signed up for the writers' group.

The first meeting of the writer's group was that Friday, only two days from when we signed up. When we entered the room the group owner greeted us and introduced us to the rest of the group. His name was Professor Bannet, but he allowed all who joined his club to call him Rob, short for Robert of course. He was an easy man to get along with, and was not intimidating to approach, he was taller than both me and Oliver, he must have been over six foot, and he was thin, not too thin, he did have some muscle which was visible and sent a message to those who would think about challenging him. An interesting man indeed. Oliver was a lot more outgoing than I when it came to talk with the other new students. In only an hour we had made an entirely new group of friends, and when I say we I really mean Oliver, I believe they only accepted me into their group because I was with Oliver. At least I had the comfort of knowing that he would never let me be singled out as we thought of each other as brothers at this point. After the first meeting we went back to the cafe we went to on the day we arrived at the university, our new friends had other plans which neither Oliver nor myself were interested in.

Since it was a Friday we did not feel as guilty in chucking down all the cups of coffee we could afford while still being able to support ourselves at university. This time I felt confident enough from the high I was getting from the caffeine to speak to Claudia properly. "How long have you worked here?" was my first question when she served us our third round of coffee, "since I was twelve, my family own the cafe and both I and my brother were expected to work here, but he decided to pursue a professional career as a chef," she said almost spitefully, "Is he the cook we met on our first day here?" added Oliver, "oh goodness no," she laughed, "he is lucky he is allowed to do so much as visit for family dinner's on Sunday. My dad was not happy when he told us he was leaving the family business. No, that is my cousin, he came here from Prussia when my brother left, and my dad offered him the position."

"where does he work now?" I added, "Simpson's in the Strand, too fancy for the rest of us but my brother always thought he was born for that kind of life,"

"I think I understand where he is coming from" joked Oliver, I laughed along with him, but Claudia did not seem to be amused. "I should get back to work, but it was nice talking to you both. Maybe I'll see you at the end of my shift," she said politely, "when do you finish?" I asked a bit abruptly, she looked at me and smiled, "I finish at four,"

"only two hours from now, maybe you could join us then?" she kept smiling and nodded at me, "okay, but I have to go now or my dad will get angry," she walked over to the customers who had just came in. Oliver stayed for an hour before he wanted to go back to the university, but I wanted to stay for Claudia, "Please, just wait an hour then leave?" I pleaded, "You'll be fine without me."

"maybe she only wanted to join us because of you,"
"I promise you that's not the case," he began to get ready to leave so I stood up as well "then I'll just come with you, we can see Claudia another day" he shot me his disapproving look, "fine, I'll stay until she finishes but then I'm off," Oliver stayed true to his word and the second Claudia came to our table he was gone.

I thought Claudia and I got along very well. I asked her about the cafe and her family, and she asked me about university, I can't express how relieved I was that she didn't ask about my own family. "What do you study?" she asked, "Oliver and I are studying law," she laughed quietly, "what?" I asked, "every time you answer my

questions you mention Oliver in some way,"
"oh, I didn't notice"
"don't worry about it," she assured, "it's adorable" I found this more of an insult than a compliment as I was always taught that men are strong and can't be "adorable", nonetheless I pretended I wasn't bothered and I continued the conversation. "What are your plans for the future? Do you always want to work in this case?" I asked, and then I realized that I must have opened up a door that until now she thought would always be closed and she liked it that way, but now it seemed she couldn't hold back. "I would like to be a journalist for the paper, but it doesn't seem realistic, my family expect me to work here and keep the cafe in the family."
"Why do you think it's not realistic? It's your life you can do anything you please with it." she looked at me as if she was disappointed in what I said, but she did not care to go on, so I dropped the subject. "How many siblings do you have?" I asked her, "just one, my older brother Joseph. He was engaged recently to an Englishwoman named Dianne; my parents don't like her too much, but I think she is okay"
"Your parent's don't like much do they," I joked and as soon as I said I regretted it because I realized how it sounded, but she laughed along with me and from this point it was like we broke the barrier and our communications going forth were comfortable, as if we had been old friends.

When I returned to the halls, I immediately went to Oliver's room like we were children again sharing our secrets and achievements. When he saw me, he smiled deviously, "so how is the love bird?" he said, I laughed. There was a weird sense of joy in my heart that I could not shake, and it kept the smile I had on my face when I left Claudia after the cafe had closed. "Don't be silly,

I'm not in love, I've only just met the woman"
"Tell that to your face when you saw her,"
"I don't know what you mean"
"Your whole face lit up like the streetlamps in the dark, and your cheeks flushed like a schoolboy who has been approached by a beautiful girl. And don't get me wrong she is a beautiful woman. And I think she might fancy you back;"
"Nonsense... why would you think that"
"There was something in her eyes when she looked at you, it was almost the same as yours but not as intense." he mocked, "I do not think she has the same interest in me as I do her, who could ever fall in love with a man like me, I am weak, I could not protect her, I could not provide her with what she deserves. Could I?"
"I think you do not look in the mirror and see yourself enough, any woman would be lucky to have you, because you are a right softy and fairly good looking, you're the dream." he mocked again, I threw a pencil at him, "Honestly Sam, just because your dad was a twat, doesn't mean you're entirely useless." he tried to lighten his statement with laughter but being reminded of Bart only made me feel guilty. "Sorry Sam"
"It doesn't matter, I think I'll head to bed. Maybe we can go round the town again tomorrow?"
"If you fancy it." I nodded to Oliver and then headed to my own room, feeling a way I was not expecting to feel when I left Claudia.

The writers club was held on several evenings of the week, Tuesday, Thursday, Friday, and Sunday. Getting to these days was like climbing a mountain, but the mountain was built from impatience and excitement. It is hard to say what the best part of the club was, whether it was the ability to share our passion for writing with others or having the excuse to create, which I soon realized was practically forbidden in a law course. Or maybe it was just Rob. He was so enthusiastic about the club and embracing the power of imagination with other young writing enthusiasts. Rob was an interesting man, he looked like he was past his forty's but did not appear to have a wife or children to account for. I was intrigued by his lifestyle, but I could not see myself being able to live this way. It appeared to me too lonely and only suited to those with the acquired taste, but at the same time I had a yearning desire for it, if I did not crave the contact of another human like we all do, I would disappear off to where no one would be able to find me, this was a longing that I could never shake, even to this day I am convinced that if I were to be able to live past the expectations, I would live alone. He set us tasks for each day we met, he created exercises to strengthen the creative part of our brains. I admired this man. He was everything I wanted to be, but more importantly he introduced me to a power that we all have but not many of us use. Whatever you choose, you can have, if you choose to fly and explore multiple continents, you can, if you choose to slay dragons in a mythical world that was created by you, you can, if you wish to transform a man into an insect you can. But of course, with everything good in the world there is limitations, none of these things can actually happen, they can only remain in your head and it can be isolating sometimes. But I thought, if I were to break the loneliness, I could live the lifestyle that I desired, one completely alone with all the time in the world to live inside my own head. This seems so much more appealing from my current situation.

I remember so vividly the first task we were set, each one of us must construct a creative piece, whether it be a short story or a poem, or a part of a play. I was so excited, more than Oliver who seemed more anxious than most about the task. This shocked me because he was always the more enthusiastic out of us both. With every task he was given he tackled it with intense concentration and ardour. I asked him what was causing his anxiety, "there is a lot of people in that group, which means there's a lot of competition, not just that, art is personal."

"Two things wrong with that sentence, it's not a competition, and art does not have to be personal"

"Sam, you've got a lot to learn. It may have not been specified that it was a competition but it's part of human nature to be competitive, when I read out my piece everyone else in that room will be judging the quality of my work and comparing it to theirs, also, art is built from expression and where there is expression there is emotion and emotion is personal" I strongly disagreed with Oliver at the time but I knew he was right, I just didn't want to be wrong. When we returned to the writer's club the next day Oliver had written a poem about growing up in a foreign country even though he was born there, or at least that is what I took from it, it was quite hard to tell really through all of the metaphors. But what a masterpiece it was. It portrayed all the emotions one would feel in Oliver's situation in words and made it incredibly difficult to still disagree with him about art being personal, I sometimes think he wrote that poem just to prove me wrong. But then I created the argument, not all art is personal, but all good art is.

After the amazing time I had with Claudia, I decided I would go to the cafe to see her after the writer's group regularly. I never specified this to her but soon enough she caught on to the routine. On occasion Oliver would come with me, but there was one day that I had planned to ask Claudia to accompany me to see the play

Macbeth in town that weekend. And the reason I planned it on the day that I did was because I knew Oliver was busy with his new friends from the football team. I bought the Monday of the same week and I had carried the tickets around with me all day as I was so excited to ask her. However, as I sat across from her in the cafe my nerves kicked me in the stomach hard and the idea made me nauseous, but I knew I had to do it. "Claudia," I began as she took a sip of her tea, "I- I- would like to ask you something?" what was going on in my head at this moment I do not know. She looked at me confused and amused at how very clearly nervous I was, and she nodded for me to continue, I took the tickets out of my pocket and slid one across the table. She looked down at it as I tried to find the words to ask her, "Would you like to come to this play with me? It's Macbeth" simple enough, yet the struggle to get those words out was powerful. She looked up at me and smiled the most beautiful and bright smile that made all my nerves disappear, "oh Sam! I have never been to the theatre before! I would love to go" she walked round to my side of the table and before I could make any move, she wrapped her arms around my neck, and we sat there in that embrace for a few blissful moments. After the cafe closed, I made my way back to the halls, eager to tell Oliver all about my evening but he was not in his room. It must have been eight or nine o'clock, but I assumed he was still out with the other men from him football team, so I went to be and resolved to tell him in the morning.

To my surprise, at early hours in the morning I was woken up by Oliver who was accompanied by the reminder to always lock my door. He shook me awake violently, my immediate thought was something terrible had happened due to the urgency in his actions and the time of day it was. This was of course not the case, but Oliver did always have a flare for the dramatic. When I had finally been shook out of my dosed state he sat at my feet and began to go on about his own romantic success of, what was now, the previous evening, "Sam you will never believe what happened to me tonight"

"Tonight? The sun is nearly up!"

"No need for specifics right now Sam. I met this beautiful woman, she's perfect! Her hair is like fire and it flows with such grace, she has these beautiful blue eyes and Sam, she's Scottish, my family will love her! It's meant to be!"

"Did you speak to her?"

"Of course, I did! How else would I know it's meant to be?"

"Well the way you are going on right now, it seems like you would think a cat was your "meant to be" if it smiled at you"

"Don't be silly," he said as he punched my arm, "It's strange you say that because I to have had a pleasant evening and I tried to tell you about it but you were not in your room."

"Tell me about your evening then and I promise I won't judge. Unlike some" I laughed and told him all about Claudia and how she agreed to go with me to see Macbeth. He already knew most about Claudia, so I probably seemed a bit infatuated as I went on about her once again. He seemed amused at my continuous rant about this woman. But then it was his turn to talk about his new sweetheart and he was no longer allowed to judge me. "Her name is Mary, I met her at the pub she works at. I don't think I have ever seen a woman so beautiful, but I didn't stare like you did, no I spoke to her. "Hello, I'm Oliver," I said to her, "Mary" she replied, but she had this devious smile, almost like she knew I fancied her, and she fancied me, but she didn't want to let on. So, I kept talking, "How long have you worked here?" I asked her, "Since I was fourteen, ma mam wanted me to learn to be independent so it was either find a job or live on the street, and you can see what one I chose," I laughed, "is it just you and your mum then?"

"In a sense, ma dad's a fisherman so he's never in, it might as well be just me and ma mam. Anyway, what do you do with your time?"

"I go to the university, I'm studying law. Is that a Scottish accent though?" she gave me a friendly but nervous smile, "so you caught on?"

"Aye, my family's Scottish as well but I was born here."

"It's not often you find a Scot in London," we laughed together, "I noticed". From there we didn't stop talking. I don't even remember what we talked about now since we talked so much. But Sam she is wonderful," he concluded, but by the end of his story I felt myself drifting off to sleep so all I could respond with was a groan. "Fine, I'll leave you be" I felt him stand up and faintly heard him leave the room.

When the day came for Claudia and I to see Macbeth, Oliver, at the last minute, decided to join us, which, I will not lie to you, I was not happy with at first, but his company with Mary was the key ingredient that made it a good night. Oliver had burst into my room that morning as I made a mental note to start remembering to lock the bloody door. "Sam! I got tickets for the play for me and Mary, and she said she would come with us!" for a moment all I could do was stand stunned at his power to somehow always make things work for him last minute and then I managed to respond, "how did you manage that?" he tapped the side of his nose, "I have my ways. I was thinking we could all go to the pub beforehand and get to know each other a bit better?"

"I don't know, Oliver, it was supposed to be just me and Claudia, and this is all very last minute-"
"Nonsense, come, I'll walk you to the cafe and you can talk to her." I gave him a look of concern, but he ignored it and left my room. I don't know why I blindly agreed to Oliver with almost everything, but I did, and I went to the cafe with him to ask Claudia if she was okay with the new plan. "Honestly, Sam you need to stop worrying about small things" he stated as we left the campus, "this isn't a small thing, she might think that her company is not good enough for me,"
"you really think too much." he laughed, "I don't" I responded defensively, I was too offended to say anything else, Oliver shot me a disapproving look, "if you say so Sammy," he changed the subject after this and I assumed it was to make me feel better before I went to see Claudia. When we got to the cafe, I asked Oliver to wait outside as I felt more confident with her when he wasn't there. She had curled her hair the night before, I noticed. She must have done it for the theatre tonight. She waved at me when she saw me, I waved back feeling slightly nervous for imposing this on her while she was at work. She ran up and hugged me tightly, I hugged her back feeling the same way about our embrace that I did the first time. After those, few blissful moments I released myself and asked her, "I was wondering if you would mind Oliver and his new friend, Mary coming with us tonight?" I held my breath as I waited for her to respond, "of course, the more the merrier they say," she smiled at me and with that smile I felt at ease, this time I hugged her. "Oliver suggested we go to the pub before to get to know each other a bit more," I said as I pulled away, "sounds like a plan," she said sounding genuinely excited. I said goodbye and I went back outside to meet Oliver, "she agreed," I said feeling ashamed that he was right, he slapped me on the back "told you so"

"whatever" I replied but I felt much more relaxed and a lot less bother by the fact I was wrong. We walked back to the campus and the next time I saw him was when we were getting ready to leave for the pub.

"I don't know what to wear!" he said once again barging into the room, "she seemed to like you in your football kit," I replied sarcastically, "don't be silly Sam, I can't go in my football stuff. The theatre is too fancy for that," I knew then that he must have been really nervous as he didn't detect my sarcasm. "what about a suit?" I suggested more sympathetically, I was wearing my own suit already, so I thought it was a fair suggestion, "a suit? She won't want me wearing a suit, that's too fancy,"
"but the football kit is too informal?"
"yes" he said firmly, I raised an eyebrow, "everyone in the theatre will be wearing a suit. Wearing anything else would only make you stand out." he seemed convinced at this point as he looked up and down at my own suit. "fine. What time are we leaving?" I looked at my clock on my desk, "you have ten minutes."
"oh no!" and he ran to his own room. He reappeared only five minutes later and this time he knocked; I opened my door to Oliver dressed in his finest suit which seemed to have altered his entire appearance. I had no words and Oliver just smirked and gleamed with pride, "Aye, you're right, she'll definitely like this," he stated as he led the way of the halls. The suit certainly made him look like a gentleman, but there are somethings such as the way he spoke and his walk, that would take a lot more work.

We met the women at the pub. They stood at the entrance waiting for us to arrive it didn't seem they spoke a word to each other that was not a hello. Mary ran up to Oliver and squeezed him, whereas Claudia

waited for me to come to her. "I'm sorry for being late, Oliver was having trouble with what to wear," I knew I wasn't late and instead the women were early, but I was always taught that the lady is always right. She laughed at my remark about Oliver. "It's okay, we were early. I didn't get a chance to properly introduce myself to Mary," she leant close to me, "she seems a bit... enthusiastic, I'm worried I might have upset her by not matching her energy,"
"don't worry about it. If she is anything like Oliver, we'll all get to know her well enough to call her friend." Oliver and Mary then came over to us, "shall we go in?" asked Oliver, "of course" I replied, taking Claudia's arm and linking it with mine, "about time," Mary joked, and we all joined in on the laughter.

The time spent in the pub was mostly just Mary and Oliver making jokes and asking each other questions, Claudia and I spent most of the time in silence, but neither of us ever felt it was uncomfortable. I suggested we left an hour before the play began so we would arrive in good time to get decent seats, Claudia agreed but Oliver felt it was excessive. "Jeez Sam! An hour! We'll be standing outside for ages before the doors open,"
"twenty minutes actually." I corrected, Oliver laughed, "what do you two thinks?" he asked the women, Mary shrugged but Claudia agreed, "I think it is a good idea, we'll have a better chance at getting good seats then. Is that your thinking Sam?" I smiled at her; it was so strange what I felt then. I felt as though I had met someone who was just as much a part of me as I was with them. You may deem me as a hopeless romantic and that I was, and I will remain for as long as Claudia is the topic of conversation. "It is exactly, my dear" I replied to her, feeling more confident and comfortable. "Very well then." Oliver said and for the first time I got

my way instead of having to agree with Oliver.

This was the first time I had been to the theatre also, but I didn't see it as such a big event in my life. I was excited, but not near as excited as Claudia, Mary, and Oliver. As we stood waiting for the doors to open, I looked at my friends in their childlike excitement. Maybe I couldn't join in their excitement because I had more of a chance to see a live performance in the theatre than they did, all I would have had to do is ask my dad and he would have paid for Claire to take us. I didn't see how far apart I was from them until I stood at the doors, but I couldn't bring this up at this moment as it would have ruined their evening. The doors opened and were among the first people to enter the performance hall. It wasn't one of the bigger theatres, but it was a decent size. There were no balconies but there must have been roughly two hundred seats on the floor. Claudia wanted to sit right at the front, and I did not deny her this opportunity. We allowed Mary and Oliver to go first down the front row, then I sat next to Oliver and Claudia next to me. The show started five minutes after we sat down and I experienced one of the most powerful moments of my life, sitting front row in a theatre in London watching Macbeth. At some point through the performance I took a quick glance over to Mary who was completely immersed in the experience and I felt a sense of pride for giving her this opportunity.

Once the performance was over Claudia had thanked me for the evening, but Oliver and Mary were not ready to end the night here. They made the proposal to us that we should go get some dinner, but none of us wanted anything fancy so we went to a chip shop that wasn't so far from Claudia's home and as I learned soon after it wasn't far from Mary's either. I was relieved they chose

a chip shop as not only was it not fancy, it wasn't expensive either. We all got fish and chips and decided to eat in the dining area that was close to empty. "How did you all enjoy the performance?" I asked, trying to break the silence, as at this point, we were all feeling lethargic after the events of the night, but the silence wasn't comfortable this time, maybe I was the only one who felt that way. I was had just become accustomed to lively conversations around the dinner table after staying so long with the McCarthy's. "I loved it! This is an experience I will never forget about!" replied Claudia. Before I could respond Mary had joined in, "if you are both students how did you afford this?" Oliver tapped the side of his nose like he did when I asked him how he managed to obtain tickets so late, I responded to Mary properly, "Oliver's parents give us money every week for food and other expenses, I had some money left over that I had been saving for nothing in particular. Oliver on the other hand, I have no idea how he always seems to manage things like this."
"well, if it gets me trips to the theatre, I won't be asking too many questions" Mary joked and winked at Claudia, she laughed with her.

When the night had ended, I walked Claudia to her home while Oliver walked with Mary back to hers. I can't speak for Oliver, but this was not a decision worth regret. For when we walked, Claudia had opened to me about her personal life a little more than she did on our first meeting together alone. "I do not want to trouble you Sam but there is something praying on my mind and I fear it has altered my personality this evening." "I haven't noticed a change at all. You are still the lovely and kind woman that I remember you as from the cafe, that first day." she smiled and looked down, so I encouraged her to continue, "However if there is something you would like to discuss, please feel comfortable to do so."

"It is about the cafe; I was so worried about the end of this lovely evening with you as I did not want you to find out where my family and I stayed."

"why not, I would never judge you on your home only your personality, and that I must say I like very much," she blushed and giggled, then continued, "my family and I, when we came here from

Prussia, we opened the cafe in hopes it would do well. However, fourteen years later and it still does not bring in the same money it puts out, so we all live in the flat above it. All three of us. It used to be four of us but when my brother got his new job, he managed to get his own house, which was a benefit, but it still isn't very big."

"Well there's nothing wrong with that. In fact, you should find pride in your family being able to keep such a wonderful and friendly place open regardless of their personal struggles, I admire you all for that. Knowing that has given me the utmost respect for you and your family and has made me certain about the feelings I have towards you" she smiled and looked up at me with small tears in her eyes. "I hope those are good feelings you have?" she joked shyly. "They are the best" I replied and then she stopped in front of me and leaned up for a kiss. This was strange yet wonderful. Never have I felt a connection so strong as that I felt with Claudia. After she pulled away, we smiled at each other and both blushed a bit, and then continued on to her home.

CHAPTER SEVEN

Unfortunately, I did not always have the financial freedom to take Claudia to the theatre, I was able to take her dinner every once and a while but not as often as I would have liked to. Claudia in no way ever made me feel as though she was disappointed with me or would prefer a man who could give her more than I could, but my insecurities always convinced me otherwise. Most of our time together was spent in the cafe that her family owned. This was because it was most convenient for Claudia and I was always taught a true man always accommodated for the lady, but more importantly it provided a great friendly and ambient atmosphere that always made me feel like I was home. On occasion we would be joined by Oliver and Mary, but they would usually be at the pub with their friends or Mary would be working. Although I enjoyed their company, Oliver was a brother to me and Mary had a great energy, I preferred it when I was alone with Claudia. It was on one of these occasions I was given what, at the time, felt like a fatal question. I should have seen it coming as she was speaking about her family a lot before she sprung it on me, but I just assumed they made her happy and that was why she was so eager to mention them whenever she could.

"Did I mention my family are Prussian?" she asked, but the topic was completely irrelevant to the topic, "you did" I responded, I tried to hide the fact that I was losing patience with her at this moment in time, "you said your family were Prussian to. When did you come here?"
"I was four, it was 1886."
"oh really! That's the same year we did! What was the date?"
"I'm not sure of the date, but I know it was summer" I could feel myself becoming impatient as I spoke about my family, but I tried to stop myself from exposing that to Claudia. "Oh, well we moved in autumn. I recently told my parents about you, they like you already" why I didn't see what was coming next is beyond me, "maybe you could have dinner with us on Sunday?" she spoke so fast I could hardly understand a word but I knew what she asked. I sat for a moment, searching hard for an excuse but could come up with none so I stalled instead. "Are you sure your parents would like that?"
"Actually, it was my dad's suggestion, he is eager to meet you,"
"You do understand I cannot offer you the same curtesy. My family is... well, we're not close," she reached out and took both my hands in her own, "I know that Sam, but maybe my family can be your family?" I saw a childlike hope in her eyes and heard it in her tone, how could I have said no?

When the day came that I should meet Claudia's family I felt a little bit ill, but not ill enough that I would not show my sweetheart my dedication to our relationship. Before I got ready and left for Claudia's family's cafe, I decided to write a short story to ease my anxieties and release all of the bad scenarios that could have happened. For the most part I was successful in easing the nerves and curing its symptoms, the ill feeling I had begun to fade, and I became a lot more confident. But when the time came that I was to be ready to leave, my stomach had twisted once again. I started to reconsider my decision to go to the dinner. I thought to myself all the excuses I could have for when I next saw Claudia. But none seemed good enough, so in spite of my nerves I went. There were several things that worried me about this evening, whether or not I would enjoy the company of her family, whether or not I would like the dinner prepared, whether or not her family would like me. So many concerns that I have never been sure if anyone else experienced. The walk felt longer than usual and every sound I heard made me jump. I had to try my hardest to swallow my fear and my heart and keep it ease until after I was back into my own room.

Relief did not come when I had made it to Claudia's, I found myself entering a small and cramped flat where three people survived, and two children managed to grow. You couldn't get to it from inside the cafe, there was an entrance on the outside which I didn't know about so Claudia had met me at the front of the cafe. When you first got in through the door you were met by a square hall which separated the rooms from each other. On one side there was the main bedroom, on the other was one smaller bedroom with a small bathroom in between. It was a simple bathroom nothing but a toilet, a sink and large metal bath. But what was most strange to me at this time was that this bath had no taps to fill it so if anyone wanted to bathe, they would have to heat up buckets of water over a fire and fill it up that way. I was shocked to see how hygienic they were despite this inconvenience which I always thought would put people off bathing altogether, it did seem like an awful amount of effort that was needed to maintain something that I found an easy and tedious task. The sitting room was straight across from the front door, it was the only entrance to the kitchen. To imagine four people living in such a small space was uncomfortable. I knew that I was very lucky to have what I had while I was growing up, however I could never imagine that this was how the other half lived.

I sat down on one of the couches and Claudia sat with me, her mother and father were sitting next to us on the armchairs they had placed on either side. In front of us was a fire which provided warmth and a serene atmosphere, the conversation was scarce but there was no awkward silence between us. This was when I found my relief. Although we did not always fill the room with speech, it was like we were learning more about each other just sitting in this silence and enjoying the peacefulness that surrounded us. "I better go check on the dinner," Ana, Claudia's mother added, "Claudia, come help me," Claudia then joined her mother in the kitchen, and I was left with her father. For the first few moments it felt intense, "What do you do Samuel?" Jakub, Claudia's father, asked, "I'm studying for my law degree sir," I replied nervously, "That's a good career. My brother was a lawyer in Prussia, but then he was drafted. Part of the reason we left Prussia was because I didn't want the decision of whether my so lives or dies to be up to some high up twat who had everything handed to him. I'm assuming your father felt the same?" I didn't know how to respond, so I thought it would be easier and more appropriate to agree, although I knew my father wasn't
thinking of me when we left Prussia. "Claudia told me you like to write?"
"uh, yes sir." I responded sheepishly waiting for all of the insults to come pouring out. "what do you write?" he asked sounding genuinely interested, I began feeling a lot more comfortable and responded to him with confidence, "I write short stories sir, horror stories

mainly."

"horror, ae? I do like horror, Poe's my favourite, have you read any of his work?"

"not much sir, it's mostly Shakespeare I read,"

"ah yes, you took Claudia to that theatre production of Macbeth. She was very happy about that; I've never seen her so excited about something before in her whole life."

"it was a pleasure, sir, I love spending time with her"

"Please, no formalities here, call me Jakub" I smiled, and we continued on talking about our favourite writers, a conversation I wished I could have had with my father.

Soon we would be joined by Claudia's brother Joseph, he was older than Claudia by three years making him twenty-one at the time and he was engaged to an English woman named, Dianne. Dianne was also joining us for the dinner, and it was clear almost halfway through the evening that Jakub did not approve of his only sons' choice in bride. As we sat for dinner the conversations had calmed from when Joseph and Dianne had first entered, this was because the food was so delightful that there was no room for anything else than the enjoyment of the dinner Ana provided but unlike most dinners I had with others this one was not so tense. All my worries had fallen at this point. From the first moment I walked through their door I was greeted with such civility and hospitality. Although they did not have the same energy that was provided by the McCarthy's, they provided a different kind of social enjoyment, which made the night so much more enjoyable and made me feel closer to Claudia. All be it I loved my time in the company of the McCarthy's, leaving Claudia's house I was so at peace with everything, they made me feel comfort in the strangest of ways and I came out a lot more relaxed than when I went in which I was not expecting. Claudia had walked me to the door and on the steps, we shared our second kiss before her father came out and put a stop to it. "Alright Claudia, in you go," he said before giving me a warm smile, "have a good night Samuel," I waved at him and then made my way back to the university.

As of tradition my first instinct was to tell Oliver of my night. However, I was greeted with the surprise of Mary answering, as I knocked on his door to give him warning of my presence. As I said before I loved Mary's company, but I did not feel comfortable opening up to her about my night with Claudia as I knew they had become close friends and that women like to gossip, so I waited until the next day where I could tell Oliver about my night and ask him how he ended up alone in his room with Mary. We were walking to the cafe after the writer's group when I introduced the topic, "Oliver, I think of you as a brother to me and I feel as though I can share anything with you"
"Well that's flattering, I think the same, Sam"
"Then you will have no reservations in telling me what you and Mary were doing in your room last night" I whispered as I did not want to tarnish her reputation and during this time it was not appropriate for an unwed women to be alone with a man behind a closed door, "Why are you so interested?" he laughed but this only made me more suspicious, "If you care about her you must be careful. You know what something like this could do to a woman's reputation."
"Ach, don't get your knickers in a twist Sam, we weren't doing anything but talking. She wanted to read some of my poems, so I thought, what better way to tell her a poem than show her the ones I already wrote."
"You two are made for each other," I mocked as I realised that they are both as careless as one another. I dropped the subject and then went on to tell him about

my night with Claudia's family. "They'll be expecting a wedding soon" he joked, "don't be silly Oliver, it's too early for that"
"oh, so you're thinking about it?"
"I was, but not too much to the extent where I'm picking out rings. But Oliver, I do believe I'm in love with the woman."
"I could've told you that last week," he replied and we both went our separate ways, I to see Claudia and he to see Mary.

The next week at the writer's club Rob had pulled me aside afterwards for a story I had written two weeks previously, Oliver wanted to go out with his friends but he offered to stay with me, I refused his offer as I didn't want him to miss out on an enjoyable evening and besides I planned to meet Claudia at the cafe after the club and I knew I was going to much later if I had Oliver waiting for me. "About this story you wrote a few meetings ago, the one you submitted to me to look at?" Robert began, I felt my nerves twist my stomach as the worries I had flooded to the surface, "Yes, is there something wrong with it?"
"Absolutely not Sam, it is brilliant. I only wish it was longer." I was dumbfounded with this response so much that it left me speechless. "I think you should submit this to The Daily Telegraph,"
"It can't be that good," I snapped, I shocked myself with this response as I don't remember thinking about it before hand. "You need to believe in yourself more, Sam. This piece is fantastic, and I have no doubt that it deserves publication. But it is up to you," he handed me the short manuscript back, "please think about it. You are a talented writer and deserve recognition." I took the manuscript and left with a lot on my mind, but I did not return it to my room as I was already late to meet Claudia.

When I got to the cafe, she did not look happy and I felt my anxiety rising with every step to the table. "Where were you?" she asked me bluntly, "I was with Rob, he read my short story," I didn't say this enthusiastically but rather disappointed which was unintentional, but it made her mood change from angry to sympathetic. "Oh Sammy I'm sorry he didn't like it," she stood up to give me a hug, I hugged her back but I of course had to tell her the true result, "He liked it, he liked it so much that he thinks I should send it to The Daily Telegraph," she released me and looked at me with a big smile on her face but then looked confused which she was right to be. "What is the matter with that? That is fantastic!"
"I don't think it's as good as he is saying it is."
"Don't be silly Sam you're a great writer"
"Well you would say that. You love me."
"And I've read your work before and think it is sensational. Please submit it. If not for yourself do it for me?" she knew I could never say no to anything she wanted because I felt guilty for how little I could give her already, so in a way I had no choice but to submit it. I did as she bid and sent my story away.

I waited over a week before I heard back from the paper, but it was worth it in the end as when they had written back they had given me some of the best news I have ever had in my whole life up until this point. I wish I had kept the letter but as time had gone on it seemed unnecessary. What it had reported back to me was that the paper loved my piece and would love to publish it in the newspaper for the next again weeks issue. I was ecstatic, I could not hold back my excitement. I told Oliver and Claudia immediately, I went to see Rob and he joined in my excitement but he couldn't help himself rubbing it in that he was right, which did not bother me as much as it would have if it were anything else because I was on cloud nine at this point. I could not believe my luck, it felt as though god had looked down upon me finally and gave me a break, from all the negativity I was forced to endure before this point. I waited eagerly for the next weeks paper to be printed. Every morning I was at the local shop, seeing whether the paper had been delivered. I had never had any interest in the news until this point. But when I found out my story would be published and my name would be given to the consumers of literature, I became ever so fond of it. Seeing my name in print was an experience that I cannot describe. I thought writing was as good as it could be, but I was wrong, having my name and my creation in print was as good as it could ever be. I got a letter shortly after from the McCarthy's which was filled with their praises. They told me that the twins loved it especially and they couldn't wait until I got home so I could write them one. When I next saw Jakub, he shook my hand, congratulated me, and told me how proud he was that his daughter had chosen a man like me. He then went on to ask about my other stories which I tried to stay as vague as possible about as I did not believe they were as good and I was ashamed of them, but the success of this one was a motivator for myself to write better stories and share them more often.

CHAPTER EIGHT

Oliver and I graduated in 1904 at the age of twenty-two. We did so well in our degree that we were among the top students of the year and were given not only a degree, but letters of recommendations from our lecturers, praising our excellent work ethic and academic achievements. This was one of the most important days of my life so of course I wanted to spend it with my own family. But no one came for me but Claudia and the McCarthy's. I wasn't ungrateful for their support, but I felt as though I was missing out on something. I didn't blame Alex for not showing up, as we hadn't spoken for six years at this point and I wasn't entirely sure she lived at the same address. In terms of my father, it didn't shock me that he neglected to attend his only son's graduation, I was certain that he was living in a constant intoxicated blur and wouldn't dare to return to reality for anything.

Claudia was the first one to arrive for the ceremony and managed to take a front row seat and save the rest of the row for the McCarthy's. One of the other men who was a part of Oliver's social circle had recognised her and pointed her out to me immediately. She waved with the biggest and brightest smile. Seeing her lifted my sunken spirits and I ran towards her. "Claudia! You are so early!"

"I know, but I couldn't wait I was so excited. Mary said she would come with me, but when I went over, she was still getting ready. She's so nervous to meet Oliver's family, she has turned into a timid child," we laughed quietly together, "really, she has nothing to worry about," I responded, "the McCarthy's are among the most accepting people I have ever met. She would be better just being herself."

"I told her that, but she didn't listen, she'll have to find it out herself. Is there someone I can talk to? I wanted to save this row for Oliver's family and Mary,"

"Claudia that is so kind of you, but I don't know if they'll let you." I looked around to see if there was any of the organizers, "that man over there, that's Rob, a good friend of Oliver and I, maybe you could speak to him?"

"okay. You better go get ready for the ceremony," she said as she hugged me tightly, "well done Sam,"

"Thank you" she let me go and walked over to Rob as I joined back with Oliver and the other men graduating today.

Only five minutes later, the other families arrived and among those was the McCarthy's and Mary. Oliver and I were shocked to see Mary when she arrived. Never had either of us imagined she could look so proper. She was usually dressed in brown or green and very rarely ventured to a different colour, she never wore an ounce of make-up either and wore her hair the way it was when she woke up that morning. But when she appeared among the crowd of the other guests Oliver and I had to look twice. She was completely unrecognisable. She was wearing a beautiful yellow dress with a white cardigan and her long hair was pinned up neatly in a bun. I had to bite my tongue, so I didn't laugh but Oliver was torn between liking the normal Mary and this new Mary. But we both had to wait before we could speak to anyone as the ceremony was about to start and we had to be prepared. Claudia looked to me and Oliver after finding Mary and we both pointed to the McCarthy's, Rob managed to reserve the front row for them. Claudia had introduced both her and Mary and led them to the seats.

Once the ceremony was over, I joined Claudia as Oliver made an official introduction between his family and Mary, he was still unsure how to take her new appearance, but I convinced him to keep his concerns to himself and wait to see how things go. "Why don't we get some lunch at the cafe?" Oliver suggested, by "the cafe" he meant Claudia's family's cafe, no one object and we all walked over there. As we sat for the first few moments Mary was silent. Only speaking when spoken to, I could tell the McCarthy's were confused as Oliver had told them about Mary in his letters and this was not the Mary they were expecting. "So, Claudia," began Creighton, "your family owns this cafe?"
"they do, they opened it in 1886 and we have never had a day when there wasn't at least one customer," I loved the way Claudia filled with pride when she spoke about her family, "I can see why, the food is lovely" replied Cromwell. "May I be excused. I must use the lady's room, Claudia, will you join me?" Mary asked, she sounded so tense and awkward, it was comical. Once both women had left Mrs McCarthy asked, "Oliver, that's not the girl you told us about. She's far too proper," Oliver looked down at his plate as his siblings sniggered, "I think she's a bit nervous, she wasn't too sure you would like her the way she is" I added, "well tell her to be herself," Mrs McCarthy demanded, but before we could say another word Mary and Claudia returned. None of us could have made it more obvious

that we were talking about them. "Is there something the matter?" asked Claudia as Mary looked down in shame, "Mary," Oliver began nervously, "please be yourself, my mum would feel much better,"
"well thank goodness for that," blurted Mary and she released her hair from the bun, "that bun was pulling so hard I thought it would have taken off ma scalp," she said to Claudia, we all laughed. We had a much more relaxing lunch now that Mary wasn't pretending.

Once the lunch was over, we said goodbye to Claudia and Mary. Claudia became emotional as we were returning to Lewes and we were uncertain as to when or if we would be returning. I promised her I'd write to her as often as possible and as soon as I was home, wherever my home would be, I would search for a job back in London and return to her. Oliver and I went back to the halls to collect our things as we were expected to have moved out of our rooms by the end of the day. We walked with the McCarthy's to the train station and made our way back to Lewes. "Where are you planning on living now Sam?" asked Mr McCarthy, I wasn't sure what to tell him, as I had thought too much into it, I only knew I would not be returning to my dad. "I was thinking about going to see Alex and maybe stay with her until I can move back to London" I replied, "oh you're going back to London? I didn't think of that," added Mrs McCarthy, "I'm hoping to go back too mum, but I'll look for a job in Lewes first and maybe move in with Mary," Mrs McCarthy started to tear up a little, "it won't be immediately mum"
"I know, but we just got you both back, and I missed you both terribly,"
"why don't you stay with us Sam," added Mr McCarthy, "just while you're on the job hunt," I wasn't sure how to respond to him, their kindness was more than anyone could have asked for and still they're offered me more. I

ended up accepting their offer and promised I would not take advantage of their kindness.

While staying with the McCarthy's the second time I was a lot more conscious of how much I took from them, whether that be food, money, or space and it motivated me every day to find a job and repay them in some form or at least to stop draining their resources. Claudia and I wrote to one another every week, but since I was unemployed, I was unable to travel to see her and although she offered to come to me, I was too proud to accept this offer. She asked me in every letter how my hunt was going, and every letter I wrote in return I would tell her of the new rejection I got. I looked for law firms mostly in London, but when I got desperate, I went to places that were no further than an hour train journey from Lewes. Every firm told me that I didn't seem interested in the position and it concerned them that I wouldn't be a reliable employee, at the time I thought they were wrong but as I reflect now, I realise they were right. After I was rejected from my dad's old firm I gave up. I was at my breaking point and I was losing all hope, especially after Oliver had moved out of his family home after making enough money from working in my dad's old firm. He stayed in Lewes, but I still felt like a failure and a burden to the McCarthy's and then he moved Mary in with him and I saw him much less than I already did due to his new job.

But then it came to me. I had much better chance of obtaining a position in a field where creativity is at its core and I could use my published story as a form of qualification. At first, I wanted to keep my new goal secret as I was worried it would be deemed not "manly" enough or people would judge me for throwing away a degree I worked four years for. But I knew with certainty that I needed this. I applied first for the news agency in Lewes, but they had no available positions so I went straight to London as I knew I would be returning as soon as I had the financial means to. I wrote four letters to four news agencies in London which portrayed my passion for imagination, creativity, and writing, and alongside that I sent a selection of my best short stories and a sample article to form a sort of portfolio. When I had done all of that I wrote to Claudia with my new plan hoping she would support me as she always did in the past. She was taking on extra hours in the cafe, so it took a while for me to get a reply but when I did, I was dumbfounded at her response.

My dear Sam,

My mother and father have been asking when you will be coming back to London. But with this news I do not know what to tell them. You have bid me to keep it a secret but I worry, and I cannot express my worries to you through letters which I have so little time to write, so must I drag these worries with me day after day until you return to me? Which now may be years? You know I will always support you my dear but this idea of yours is a gamble, and you have never been a gambler. I don't think I understand, why you have turned your focus to a career path you haven't spent four years working towards. If you could explain to me then maybe I could support, you are more. You know I always want the best for you, but I don't feel this is what is best. It seems drastic and out of character.

What does Oliver think? Mary told me he is now working in your father's old firm, maybe he could get you a position with him.

I hope to hear back from you soon my dear, I miss you terribly.

Sincerely, Claudia

The next letter I wrote to her I explained everything, and although she did not seem to fully understand she supported me and tried hard to help me anyway she could in my search for a career in the creative industry.

It wasn't until the summer of 1905 when I finally had a break-through in my search thanks to Claudia and her brother's wife. She wrote to me frantically, as I could see from her handwriting, about an editing position that had opened in Dianne's brother's agency. My heart jumped at every word I read. It felt like the beginning had finally came for me and I would soon be on my way to a life worth living. The interview process was not challenging, the most challenging part was the portfolio they requested as the one I sent was not exactly what they wanted. Instead they wanted an edited piece of one of the articles in the paper that was published previously. I feared that they may be trying to trick me in some way, but I went with it regardless. When I went to the interview with my portfolio, they seemed impressed and the same week I received a letter noting my acceptance into their editorial team and when I would start. My first thought from this point was to tell Oliver and then write to Claudia, and when I did, I got the most encouraging response, as well as several questions from Oliver and his family. "This is just fantastic Sam," said Oliver's father, "We're so proud of you both," Oliver's mother added when she brought through a tray of tea for us. "So, when do you start?" Oliver asked "Next week. For the first few months I hope you will let me stay a little longer until I

can afford somewhere in London" Oliver's mother was the first to respond, "You're going all the way to London, Sam? Don't you want to stay in Lewes?"
"Of course he doesn't, mum, he wants to be closer to Claudia, I'm sure he told you he was going back to London anyway mum?" she sat silent holding back her tears and to cheer her up Oliver tried to make a joke out of the situation, but I could tell I was upsetting his mother. "I mean no offence; I will of course come back to visit. You have all become like a family to me, it would only be right." Mrs McCarthy came over and held me tightly like my own mother used to. I know a lot of you will be wondering if I forgot about my poor sisters at this point in my story. I didn't. I felt however that she wanted nothing to do with me and at this point it was easier to put them out of my mind. But I promise you that Alex and Hanna were never truly out of my heart.

On my first day Claudia met me at the train station and walked me to the agency, I think she was more excited than I was. My new boss greeted me at the door. He was a short man, but he was strong. I guess it would only be fitting for a disadvantaged man to make his own advantage. His name was Mr. Alton Scott, but he preferred to be referred to as just Alton. He was surprisingly friendly, I should probably clarify that I wasn't expecting any social interaction from him at all, but my assumption was proven wrong when he greeted me with a formal introduction and a handshake. "Good morning sir, I believe you must be Mr. Samuel Nowak?" he had a strong London accent which did not match his fancy appearance, "I am sir, and how may I address you?"
"My name is Alton Scott. But you may call me Alton, I find it brings a much better working environment when we all address each other by first names, I hope you

agree?"

"Of course si- Alton" I was nervous to reply because he sounded like there was an underlying seriousness to his question, then he said, "that's good or else you wouldn't be allowed to work here" he laughed so hard I thought he would explode but I couldn't help feeling he meant it. He made me nervous at first, but I brushed it off to get through the day. As an editor for this paper I spent my long shifts looking through articles and submissions from people like myself who had a passion for writing and submitted their work to the paper. During these first few months I was travelling back and forth from Lewes to London on the train and walking from the train station to my new job and the McCarthy's house. When my first wage came in, instead of looking for a house I bought Mr McCarthy's car from him. He had arthritis and it had spread to a large portion of his body making it harder for him to drive. Thankfully because I knew him, I got it for cheap. The car did set me back a lot which left the consequence of living with the McCarthy's for another year before I could have my own home. I'm sure this pleased Mrs McCarthy as it meant I was living in Lewes a little longer than I had planned. Claudia wasn't too happy with the decision as she wanted me to move back as soon as possible, but of course her opinion did not make a difference as by the time I had told her the deed was done.

When the time came for me to move permanently to London, I felt a sense of freedom and strange unfamiliar relief. It was not that I did not enjoy the company of the McCarthy's, or appreciate their help and civility, in fact to this day I still don't know how I could repay them. Once I was settled into my two-bedroom home I soon learned the consequences of living independently, it was isolating and although I used to think I would be able to handle it, I was surely proven wrong after the first week. I invited Oliver over as often as I could and offered him the guest room so he could save the late journey home. He did not always take my offer because he has always had a close attachment to his own home and Mary, as I believe I have previously stated. The only time Claudia and I spent together was when Oliver and Mary were visiting, or I was at the cafe. Living alone was beneficial in terms of my career as being at work was the only time, I was obligated to spend outside of my house, so I made the most of those days by putting my all into it and doing over time regularly. I was in London almost a month before I was invited to dinner at Claudia's family's home once again. I felt guilty for accepting this time as it would have been more appropriate for them to dine at my house, but I didn't feel it was fit for company that wasn't my friends. When I arrived at Claudia's none of them held any judgement in their words for how long it had taken me to see them, but I still felt it in their expressions. I could feel their burning questions about why I have not invited them to my new home for dinner and why I don't seem to be enough for their daughter despite my past wealth and first impression. They were too polite to make this clear of course. Once again Ana's dinner was lovely and once again, I spoke most of the night with Jakub about writing. This was also the first time they had spoken to me personally since my story was published in the paper, so I received many congratulations from them.

After dinner, Claudia and I took a walk to the park that we occasionally went to after I moved. It was beautiful during the spring which it was currently, especially when the moon was full and shining down on it. This is where I made her a promise, "Claudia, I know I must disappoint you at this point-"

"Sam! What on earth would make you think that?"
"I have come from wealth and should be able to provide that to you and your family, it is no secret that so far I have failed you as both a man and a potential husband, but Claudia, if you choose to stay with me, and persevere through my journey I promise you I will achieve great things and through those things I will be able to provide you everything you could ever imagine, a home, new dresses, jewellery, anything you please, all my success will be yours. What I want to ask you is... will you be my wife?" she began to cry and nodded, I was shocked she said yes as so far I had given her nothing, I didn't get on one knee and I didn't give her a ring and yet she still wanted to be my wife. Nothing could have made me happier in the world at this point. "I don't have a ring yet, but I will get one for you when I get my next wage"
"Sam... I can't believe this. I am so lucky. I'm speechless"
"I am the one who is lucky, I can't believe you said yes" she reached up for a kiss and we stood there under the light of the moon for a few blissful moments. I walked her home and she had the biggest smile on her face, it eased my anxieties thinking that she had faith in me. After I walked home myself, I couldn't sleep. I was both exuberant and worried, I was over the moon that she said yes but it then hit me, *how the hell am I going to pay for a wedding,* I had then made the plan on how I would save and to do so it meant I would have to continue take on extra working hours which I didn't mind really. I was just hoping at this point that she'd wait for me to save. As I slept, I dreamt of her in a white dress walking down an isle as I waited for her. I knew then she would make a beautiful bride.

My dream was interrupted when in early hours of the morning I was awoken by a knock on the door which gave me an instinct that it was one bringing bad news or perhaps evil with its source. When I answered I was greeted by a nurse who had a grave expression. She handed me a letter without giving me her name or any formal greeting, she handed me the letter and said "I am so sorry" her voice was filled with sorrow but she seemed to have experienced a lot of sorrow from her ability to remain stoic. She then turned around and scurried off without allowing me a second to gather the situation in my thoughts. I closed the door and went to my sitting room where I planted myself on my armchair and held the letter out in front of me with caution as if I was holding a stray animal. My hands shook as I opened the folds and my thoughts went immediately to Alex and Hanna, guilt then filled my body and twisted my stomach into knots making me nauseous. When I had revealed the writing of the letter inside, I skimmed to see if Alex or Hanna were mentioned and to my delight, they weren't so I felt more at ease to go on, but the news was still not pleasant. The letter read.

Dear Samuel Nowak,

I am writing on behalf of your father who has been repeating your name since he was brought to us last Thursday. I am sorry for being the bearer of bad news here, but he has fallen severely ill and will not make it past the week. We do not yet know what has caused this abrupt illness and unfortunately the symptoms are not familiar to us. He has asked to see you and your sisters as soon as it is convenient to you all. I have sent a letter to Aleksandria like this one. I hope you can find the time to visit him as he truly doesn't have much time left and it would be of the best interest for you all to meet him at the hospital soon.

Sincerely, Nurse Anabelle Emsworth,

Lewes Victoria Hospital

CHAPTER NINE

After reading the letter I sat for a moment on my couch, or what was supposed to only be a moment. I ended up sitting like this for an hour and what made this situation worse was I was supposed to in work at the end of that hour, but I was in a haze. Time had abandoned me, and I was completely unaware of its existence. Every second I sat there longer I could feel my body getting heavier and heavier and eventually found myself slumped on my couch. Not long later, or at least what I thought was not long there was a second knock on my door. But there was not an ounce of my body that cared who was there, I knew if we were acquainted enough they would walk in and although I would usually be embarrassed for anyone to see me like this I was too deep into my haze to care. After becoming aware of the knock, I realised I hadn't blinked in a long time and my eyes were too dry to do so now. It wasn't until Alton, my boss, was standing in front of me that I managed to force my eyes closed, but they didn't open again.

I woke up again in bed, with Claudia sitting on a chair beside me reading a book and Oliver talking to someone at my bedroom door. "Sam you're awake!" Claudia began, I saw Oliver and the stranger come towards me, the stranger had asked me questions, but I couldn't understand him. "What?" I asked, trying to make sense of what I had just heard. "Do you know your name?" the stranger asked, "Samuel Nowak" I replied, he then turned to Oliver, "he should be fine. He went into a severe shock but seems to have recovered now. Maybe let him rest for the time being and slowly integrate him back into his old routine," Oliver nodded and the stranger left, "My dad, is he-"

"No Sam, Mary went to get an update for you, he's still here with us. You have plenty of time to go see him... if that's what you want" I stayed silent. "Alton has given you time off, he said for you to take as much time as you need," Claudia added, "what happened to me?" I asked as I tried to raise myself up out of bed, "Alton got worried that you weren't in since you've never missed a day before. When you didn't answer the door, he got really concerned and tried the door. Good thing you always forget to lock it ae? Or you would have had no door." Oliver chuckled but I had no energy to laugh with him, "well when he got in he said you were completely unresponsive, he said he screamed at you and it was like you didn't hear him, but you were looking right at him, then you lost consciousness and he ran to get the doctor. He wanted to stay to make sure you were alright but once Claudia came to get me, I told him you would do better if you weren't reminded of work, sorry about that."

"How long have I been asleep?"

"Only a day Sam, doctor said you've to stay in bed as well," Oliver replied as we gently stopped me from getting up, "but I have to work,"

"didn't you just hear Claudia; you've been given time off. It's alright to take a break sometimes, especially when you spend your entire time working. You're not in trouble, Alton is completely understanding to your situation, it's alright." I did what he said, but not because I wanted to but because it felt like my body wanted to.

Once I had fully recovered from the shock, I went back to trying to decide whether to see my dad. I did not discuss the letter with Claudia although I knew her moral guidance would have been useful at this point in my life, at the same time I felt as though this was a burden I must carry on my own. The next couple of nights I spent awake, pacing back and forth trying to drown myself in work that I requested Alton to give me in hopes that it would distract me or even provoke a decision or some moral inspiration. Days were going quicker than usual, and I knew I was running out of time, so I decided to go. I thought that I would rather regret seeing him than not at all when it is too late. At this point I strongly resented the hospital, first my mum died here and now my dad, I can't find any reason to think of it anything else other than cursed and evil. I kept my decision about seeing my father to myself. I feared their sympathy and would only resent their support, so I thought it would have been better to keep it to myself. Walking up to the entrance of the hospital made me sick. I felt as though I was walking towards my own death, although the nurses and doctors had tried to make it as joyful as possible to keep up the spirits of the ill and those who care about them, this couldn't do as much for me. As I went through the white halls, I felt them mocking me, I did not belong among the purity of these people, but neither did he. It seemed an injustice to the world for such a wicked being to be treated with such kindness and respect. They were so naïve to the monster they were treating, I bet he loved that.

I was shocked to see both Alex and Hanna sitting by his bed, Hanna looked like she was praying while Alex held his hand. Hanna I was not so surprised as she was just so young and she was twelve then and could have come on her own but at the same time I expected Alex to have told her about the evil he brought to our lives in such brutal detail. I knocked before I entered as I didn't want to impose on their grief, Alex looked up at me and then down to Hanna who was now almost a young a woman. It was seeing them that made me emotional. Hanna looked up to me with empty eyes. She seemed mesmerized by me, and at the same time not seeming to see me at all, she appeared to be so far away from all of us in the room, as if she was in a world of he own that only she knew how to get to. "May I sit?" I asked Alex, and she looked up to me with anger, but instead said, "He is your dad to, you can do as you wish, not that you need me to tell you that," despite her passive aggressive comment which unjustifiably angered me, I sat down anyway on the other side of our dad. I did not cry neither did Hanna, but Alex continued to shed a tear for our him. We sat in silence until he took one last deep breath in, and out, we knew then he was gone, and although my sister felt grief, I felt relieved that the world would be rid of this monster. The nurse took us through the after death procedures and routines and gave us some addresses for undertakers, it seemed inappropriate to be talking about his burial so soon after his passing but it must be done, if it was up to me and me alone I would not bury him, I would burn him so he may return to the place he always belonged.

It was a difficult situation, but I decided to stay to comfort my sisters. At first Alex was hesitant and wanted to resist my attempt, rightfully so, but then she accepted, and I was grateful. I took them both for lunch where I spoke to them about my decision to abandon them and tried to form an apology to Alex most of all. "I cannot begin to imagine what it has been like for you two, to grow up without a strong male figure or female role model in your lives, and part of that is my fault, for that all I can say is sorry as I cannot take away your pain or change the past no matter how much it grieves me, I hope you both can find it in your hearts to forgive me, and we can begin to mend our relationship as it is only us now from this mess of a family."

"Samuel" she began "you were not fully in control of the situation we were put in, although you did not help much either. I think I can forgive you if you prove to me you are more than the man who left us, we need our brother not an unreliable worm."

"I promise, I have changed, but of course only time will prove that," I reached over to Alex's hand and then addressed Hanna, "what about you Hanna? Hanna?" Vacant! She was completely vacant. A hollow shell in human form, was this my doing? Alex nudged Hanna and Hanna looked at her confused as if she didn't remember how she ended up where she was. Alex looked at me and nodded, she didn't see any reason to go through the conversation with her.

After this we discussed what had happened while we were apart like everything was normal. Alex had met a man who promised her one day he would marry her and provide the best life he could for both her and Hanna. I was suspicious, but Alex seemed convinced that he was the one who would move heaven and earth for her. I wanted to meet him immediately, but I did not feel I had the right to push her at right then due to my long absence and failure as a brother. I told them, or rather I told Alex about Claudia and our recent engagement, Alex herself was eager to meet her just as much as I was to meet the man, she told me about. I decided to organise a dinner with her, Hanna, Claudia, and Mr. Andrew Melvin which was the man my sister was talking about. This would allow us all to meet our new in-laws and perhaps re-build our relationship. I then

went on to ask her about Hanna. "She's been doing very well. I don't think I've mentioned yet but Liz took me on as her accountant as I seemed to have shown her my skill with numbers. So, I have been given a bigger wage and I've hired a tutor who specialises with students who may need a little extra help. The tutor says she's a very talented artist, but I don't know enough about Art to give my own opinion"
"Well that's fantastic, you used to be good at art yourself, do you remember? you must bring some of her work to the dinner. Claudia loves art." she blushed a little which answered my question but then went on, "I will, I'm sure Hanna will have some new pieces done by then, it practically occupies her life" we laughed together but I was so proud of both of them. They were special women.

The dinner would be at a restaurant in London, I felt bad for making them travel so far and offered to pick them up, but Alex said she and Andrew would be travelling together on the train. My second concern of the evening was that they wouldn't be able to afford to eat at the restaurant we had chosen but Alex then reassured me that Andrew would be willing to pay for both her and Hanna. I booked the table for the next again night, after we discussed these details, at six o'clock sharp for the five of us. I then went to see Claudia and asked her if she would like to join me, she seemed shocked at the request but delighted none the less. "I would love to meet your sisters Sam! I had no idea you were talking again."
"Yes well, I was going to shield you from my tragedy but due to the circumstances you should know, my dad passed, we were not close, none of us were to Bart, in fact it is a very long, tiring and depressing story that I do not wish to get into at this time, I hope you can respect this?" instead of replying she put her arms

round my neck and kissed me, there was something special about her embrace that I felt every time, something comforting that made me believe the world was a safe place and not full of evil as I had learned up until this point.

I would like to think the dinner went well. I tried not to scare the poor man away, but I did interrogate him relentlessly with my questions for the first twenty minutes of the evening. I discovered he was a doctor and was a little older than myself. His family had been very wealthy which meant that he had a rather large inheritance after their passing and would soon inherit his uncle's property in the countryside, which he hoped to move into with my sisters. Money cannot buy love or respect, but I hoped Alex would find someone who would provide the lifestyle she deserved and has worked hard for and he seemed qualified for that. After the dinner, I found a moment with Alex alone in which I thanked her for forgiving me and joining me this evening, I told her I thought Andrew was the right man for her and I wanted nothing more than for her to be happy and satisfied with the life she chooses, whether that be with him or without. Then I showed her the surprise I had for Claudia. When I told Alex that I had proposed to Claudia I did admit that I hadn't bought her a ring yet so before the dinner I went into town alone to look at engagement rings. I picked out one that was extravagant but still in the budget. The only thing left to do was to surprise her with it. I am a man of tradition, and although I, in a sense, proposed to Claudia before, I wanted to give her a traditional proposal. Therefore, I went to her father when she was at work and asked his permission, his reaction was surprising to say the least. "I was wondering if you were going to ask me" he said laughing and shaking my hand, "of course! I've always wanted my daughter to have the best life possible and if she found man that could provide that life for her I could die a happy man, and Samuel, I knew from the first moment you were going to give her everything I wanted for her. Of course, you have my blessing," I was honoured to have this man's permission to marry his daughter. Once I purchased the ring, I started working on my plan on how I would propose this time properly. I hoped after the dinner we'd walk through the park once again and I could give her a proper proposal under the moonlight. When I showed Alex the ring, I saw her eyes widen and she hugged me tightly, it was strange to be hugging my sister for the first time in almost a decade. "She will love it, Sam. And she is so beautiful, you both seem to be a match made in heaven."

"Thank you, Alex. I am so incredibly glad to have you back in my life to share this moment with, honestly, I am lucky to have you as a sister and I will spend my life repaying you for your kindness."

"Don't be silly Sam, she makes you the man you should be. I can see that you've changed. There is no need to make it up to either of us. Just stay with her and continue being the way you are." we all said our goodbyes and went our separate ways.

I convinced Claudia to walk through the park before she went home, and this is where I asked her. I did the traditional, get on one knee and present her the ring, and I said to her, "Claudia, I love you more than words can ever portray. You have made me a better man and the best version of myself. If I had not met you, I do not know where I would be. And for those reasons I want to spend my life with you as my wife."

"Sam," she said through tears, "You really did not need to go through all of this. But I am so grateful that you did. Of course I will marry you" I jumped back to my feet and embraced her, "I'm so glad you said yes again,

I fear your father would have been incredibly disappointed if you didn't" we laughed at this silly joke and here is where this evening ended.

CHAPTER TEN

Claudia and Alex started planning for the wedding that weekend. I had invited Alex and Hanna to stay in the spare room, but Alex didn't want Hanna to get in the way and decided it would be best to leave her with their neighbour. I hadn't told Oliver about my engagement as it had slipped my mind after everything that had happened, but I was reminded about it by Claudia. I usually met Claudia at the cafe and I walked back with her to my house, it was on one of these mornings that she asked me if I had spoken to Oliver yet, "I was wondering if you have written to Oliver about the engagement yet? I would love Mary to come and help Alex and I with the planning,"
"You know, it completely slipped my mind. I can't believe I haven't told him yet."
"Don't worry about it, you have had a lot of things to deal with. Would you like me to write to Mary?"
"No, no. He would lose his mind if I didn't tell him." I pondered a way to tell Oliver for a moment, "I will go see him today, it's probably better that I do it in person now I've waited so long."
"Well you're not going, now are you?"
"Right. I'll wait for Alex to arrive and then I'll go see him. You both can manage for a bit without me? I'll be back by dinner"

"Of course we'll manage. We've been planning this wedding ourselves all week anyway." we laughed together and then continued on back to my house. Alex joined us an hour after we arrived and after seeing they were comfortable, I left to tell Oliver. Thankfully, he wasn't too aggrieved with my timing. "Congratulations Sam!" he rejoiced, "maybe you can inspire Oliver" Mary added, Oliver ignored the comment, "what's the date?" he asked, " we haven't decided yet, but Claudia and Alex, are planning it all now, Claudia has asked me to recruit your help Mary,"
"I would love to help!"
"Wait, who is Alex?" Oliver interrupted, "my sister Aleksandria," I replied nervously, he looked at me stunned, "I spoke to her and Hanna when I visited Bart in the hospital. We went for dinner and are trying to rebuild our relationship." I felt shame as I spoke, "I am so happy for you Sam." Oliver replied, lowering his voice, "Thank you. Maybe you both could come with me today and stay in the spare bedroom?"
"We would love to," Mary stated, she went to pack their things while Oliver and I discussed other events that happened while we were apart.

They had stayed with me full time for two months during the planning and then went back home the night of the wedding. There was a day that Oliver and I were at Claudia's cafe when he revealed to me his own plans to move to London. I encouraged him to do so, as when I had come here, I felt my life had taken a positive change. "It would be fantastic if you moved to London. I'm sure Mary would love to be closer to her family and it would be great to see you more often,"
"The only thing holding me back right now is my mum, not that she's doing it intentionally,"
"I'm sure she would be happy for you regardless of where you are, it will be hard for her in the beginning,

but she has the twins. Have they got any plans for their future?"

"Nolan has no clue what she wants to do, Rylan wants to be a builder, like my dad but when he went to work with him, he didn't do much and struggled taking even the simplest instructions."

"Well sounds like they'll both be close enough for your mother to bear one more child moving away"

"It's just sad to think the majority of her children have decided to take up lives so far away from her, after all she's done for us all"

"It's a mothers duty to raise their children to be able to go out into the world and stand alone, against all that might hold them back or try and harm them in anyway." he fell silent so I changed the subject to something more positive. "How are you and Mary doing? Should I be expecting wedding bells for you both any time soon?"

", I do have plans to propose to Mary soon, but I want to move here first and find us a better house. But yes, hopefully in the next few months we'll be engaged."

"I am so happy for you Oliver! Look how far we both have come since we were young boys! You a lawyer and I an editor, both with women that make us proud to know them. Who would have seen this coming?" we laughed, "certainly not me, I would have bet on the twins getting here before us."

I saved enough by the winter and we were married in the next summer. The week of the wedding was much worse than the chaos that was involved in planning it. Claudia seemed so stressed about the day that I was almost convinced she no longer wanted to get married in the first place. I was too busy to ease her stress as I had one more surprise for my wife to be. I felt it appropriate that a newlywed couple had their own home not one previously owned by one half of the couple, so it would free of old memories, and neither would feel they had anymore right to it than the other. A fresh canvas to create all new memories, a new life together. I wanted to wait until the night of the wedding to show her my secret project, so I made up every excuse I could to Claudia, in order for me to go see the house in discretion and help the decorators with as much as I could. It was a decent sized house, three bedrooms, a kitchen, a sitting-room, and a bathroom. Thankfully, I was in the habit of taking extra shifts at work already, so the process of saving proved to be a much easier task than expected. I became more acquainted with Claudia's family during this week as well since I recruited Claudia's mum to help me find the best décor and furniture for the house. Claudia's own sister-in-law, although insulted she was not invited to be a bridesmaid, had helped through the planning of the house. They knew her tastes more intimately than I, so it only seemed right they be involved. When I revealed to her dad my plans to surprise her with our own home. He offered on several occasions to help with the first payment, but I insisted that I wanted to do it all on my own, and without having to explain it, he understood almost immediately. When the house was finally finished, I was amazed at how fantastic it looked and I knew that every penny I spent was worth it. It was in the neighbouring street to that of her family's cafe, I thought she would have preferred to be close to her family as they have never been apart. It had a reputation of being a friendly neighbourhood and the school was ranked one of the best in London. Overall, I was convinced she would love it.

The wedding day proved to be one of the greatest days of my entire life. Everyone looked amazing but no one could have competed with the beauty of Claudia on this day. As she walked down her beautiful white dress, she looked like an angel sent to save me from myself. As we said our vows each syllable made my soul lift higher and higher, and I couldn't believe I was this lucky. After the ceremony we celebrated with a dinner with all our friends and family. It proved to be a small event as all our friends were part of the ceremony and we didn't have many other family members left to fill a hall. All the McCarthy's attended however and made up for the lack of guests. Claudia was delighted with the final surprise of the night. She was shocked that I would go to this length for her and that I could afford it. I didn't want to waste time explaining how I managed to do this for her, but I did give credit to her sister-in-law and her mother as they were a big help.

For the next few days, we had many visits from friends and family, but most often we had visits from Mrs McCarthy. I have had a sudden realization; I have gotten this far and not told you the names of either Mrs or Mr McCarthy. Well since you should be familiar with them now although you may have never met them in person, which I must say is very unfortunate for you, it is most likely appropriate to tell you their names. Mrs McCarthy's first name was Aileen and Mr McCarthy's first name were Brendan. Aileen, to my surprise felt it her duty to make sure we were both comfortable in our married life. She would convince, or rather blackmail, poor Brendan into taking her all the way to London and on some occasions rent them a room for the night in the bed and breakfast nearby. This worked very well for Oliver who was still fiddling with the idea of moving to London himself so Mary could be nearer to her family, so this allowed for him to look for jobs and available houses in the area. Claudia's mother was involved a lot in our married life also. Sometimes she would run into Aileen while she was at the house and the two would sit in our kitchen with cups of tea gossiping away like old

friends. Aileen and Brendan were very good to me in my younger years, and when the conversation came up with Claudia as to how I saw the McCarthy's in relation to me, I told her they were closer to a family than my family was but she was not satisfied with this response.
"Really, Claudia it is such a tiring story and rather tragic, it is not worth getting into"
"I just want to know what I should refer to Aileen as when my mother asks. She asks me constantly why she is over so much if she is just your friends' mother, it is an awkward conversation when you don't know the answer and I'm not as good as avoiding conversations like you are"
"Aileen is like a mother to me, and her husband like a dad, so if you must define my relationship with Aileen to your mum, tell her she is my mum, which would make her your mother-in-law" I said as I pulled her close to me and kissed her on the forehead in a sly way to divert the conversation.
Once we were settled into our new house Alex and I organized to meet once a week in a cafe in Lewes where we would get lunch and catch with one another. In one of our meetings she brought with her the worry she had surrounding Hanna. Andrew wanted to get married and move her in as soon as she would allow him, but for as long as Hanna was proving to be a challenge, she held back from her own happiness to provide for her. I tried to encourage her to seek professional help for Hanna, but she refused as she didn't want Hanna to be the subject of any judgement. I sympathised with Alex but at the same time I could not help but judge her for causing so much trouble to herself. I went as far as offering to pay for the help myself and suggested finding someone with a similar experience of caring for people with the same unusual struggles as Hanna. "Alex, I see your kind heart more than anyone in this world will. I know you feel

responsible for her but please think of yourself for once. It is not selfish to sometimes allow a moment for you."

"I allow many moments for me, and in those moments, I leave her with the neighbour."

"But you do not take long in returning, I know this because the neighbour herself has told me she wishes you would take some time off"

"I cannot allow her to be the subject of prejudice and hate. She is just seventeen."

"Most girls her age, in a position like hers would be out working, you were younger than that when you started."

"I had a very unique circumstance,"

"Nonetheless Alex, you cannot sacrifice your life because of Hanna. It is not good for either of you. You will be missing out and Hanna will be so sheltered from the world that when you and I... are no longer here, she will have no idea how to handle herself. If money is an issue, I can discuss with Claudia about pulling some together to help you."

"Money is no issue; Andrew has already offered to help with Hanna's care."

"And I'm assuming you turned him down as you are with me."

"She is my sister; I took on the responsibility to leave our home and start anew. It was not her fault, or her choice it was mine, and whatever consequence that choice had is also mine, and mine alone." "But those who care for you as I and Andrew do, it's would be a sin to sit back and watch you allow yourself to suffer." "What makes you think I am suffering?"

"How can you not be when you are sacrificing so much for someone else and have since you were very young?"

"She is our sister"

"Yes she is *our* sister, so let me take her, I'm sure Claudia and I will be able to work out a routine around her, and it will allow you to take a break and proceed with the wedding that you both have been wanting since you met."

"I appreciate the offer, but I cannot let you do that, now can we change the subject?" I was slightly relieved she said no, as I wasn't entirely sure how Claudia would have reacted to having Hanna in her state living with us. Especially when we are trying for a baby, it would have proved to be quite a challenge.

CHAPTER ELEVEN

In 1909 Oliver did eventually move to London with Mary. They bought their house across the street from ours and just like Oliver had said they were engaged in the same week after they moved. I was grateful I didn't have to be that involved in this wedding planning as I don't think I would have coped with the chaos it brings again. Just like Oliver did for me, I helped him escape from it all as Mary and Claudia dominated the house with all sorts of nonsense that goes into a wedding. I must give them credit however, they did a wonderful job with the wedding and all their hard work went into creating a wonderful day, not just for the bride and groom but for all their guests as well. They spent their honeymoon abroad in Rome and when they came back, they gave us the great news that they were expecting. It seemed like no time at all for them when it was taking so long for us to finally have the family we craved. I could see the toll it was taking on Claudia when Mary and Oliver came to us the day after they got home from their honeymoon, no more than a month after their wedding. She acted as the happy and supportive friend, but when she was alone, I found her curled up in bed drowning in tears. "My dear! What is the matter? Aren't you happy for Mary and Oliver?"

"Of course, I am. But why can't that be us? Why must I

be the one who cannot bear a child? I am failing as a wife and a woman; how can you even look at me?"
"Claudia, there is plenty of time for a family. We must keep trying. It will happen for us soon." I gently brought her limp body close to mine and held her tight. To see my poor wife be in so much pain felt like a bullet, but nonetheless I had to stay strong for her. She was running out of hope, but I could not. She needed me.

The next time I saw Alex I couldn't help but open to her about the struggles Claudia and I were having. I shouldn't have been surprised at Alex's response, she was always kind and supportive, "you both shouldn't worry so much, it will happen when it happens. If you force it, it's less likely to happen."
"I know Alex but it's taking such a toll on Claudia, she feels as though she has failed me," she raised an eyebrow at me, "I would never say anything of the sorts to her, she's my wife. She could never disappoint me,"
"Okay. Well maybe me and her could go out as a sort of girls day and I can convince her to stop worrying about it so much."
"Absolutely not, she would kill me if she knew I spoke to you about this,"
"She doesn't have to know, I'll convince her to tell me on her own," she gave me a sly smile, "very well, if you think you can help her and you don't mind then I don't think it will be a too bad,"
"of course, I don't mind Sam, she's family now" I stood up and hugged her in gratitude and then I went on to ask her about Andrew and Hanna. "How is Hanna?" I began, she lowered her voice and leaned in, "she is getting worse. Our neighbour has warned me she might not be able to cope much longer with her, she's having tantrums and getting violent. The neighbour thinks she's possessed, she says she has a strength she has

never seen in a girl of her build."

"That's nonsense, she's not possessed Alex. But she might need professional care?"

"No. I will not allow our family to endure anymore shame, especially through Hanna. She needs me and only me," I thought it best not to argue with her, so I changed the subject to Andrew, and I saw her entire countenance change almost immediately. "He is doing well; he is also to inherit his uncle's property in the countryside in Lewes. When he does, he says he wants me and Hanna to move in with him,"

"That's great, Alex. I'm so glad you have found someone who can give you so much, you really deserve it."

"Thank you, Sam,"

Alex stayed true to her word and she invited Claudia out on a "girls' day" that weekend. Much to my surprise Claudia had come home with a whole new perspective on the situation. When she came home that evening she was glowing with joy, "I've had such a wonderful day today with Alex," she rejoiced as she walked through the front door with a shopping bag in each hand, "she is great isn't she?" I chuckled, "well of course she is,"

"She gave me some wonderful advice today and I no longer feel out of sorts."

"I'm so glad Claudia, why don't you tell me what you talked about?" she laughed, "how about some tea instead?" I sighed, "very well then."

The Monday before I was due to see with Alex next, I had an unexpected visitor. Andrew Melvin had knocked on my door during one of my days I had taken off to be with Claudia. He brought the unfortunate news of his uncle succumbing to his illness and sadly passing, "Hello, Sam," he said awkwardly, "Hello... Andrew?"

"My uncle, unfortunately passed away last night,"
"Oh, I am so sorry to hear that, Claudia, make some tea for Andrew will you, he has just lost his uncle," I will not lie, I was incredibly confused as to why he was telling me about his uncle but grief does make us do strange things so I did not question his motives. "Do come in," I led him to our sitting-room, and we were soon joined by Claudia soon after with tea and biscuits. "It is unfortunate, but it means I have inherited his property that is just outside of Lewes in the countryside. It's a large estate on the way to London, you may have seen it?" when Alex told me Andrew was inheriting his uncle's estate, she neglected to mention how big it was. I of course knew that Andrew's family was wealthy, but this property was no smaller than a mansion, "I have seen it now I remember, a beautiful estate from the outside"
"It is beautiful inside as well. I spent a lot of my childhood at the property, so it is sentimental to me in a way. The reason I am here, is because I would like to ask Alex to marry me, and to have both Alex and Hanna come live with me at the estate. When I spoke to Alex before about us being married, she said she wanted me to have your permission, since unfortunately your father is no longer in your lives." I was shocked to hear that it was Alex that had said she wanted him to have my blessing before he committed to the proposal. But of course, I gave it willingly. This man that my sister has chosen to be her life partner and the one to give her the life she deserves was respectable in every manner. It would be cruel to deprive Alex of him. Once I told all of this to him, he told us his plan for proposing. "She has always wanted to see the river Thames," he began "but I thought I'd do one better. I have hired a sailor to take us out on a little rowboat like they do in Venice, which I plan on taking her to on our honeymoon. But as we sail down the river Thames, I

will ask her to be my wife." he then pulled a little velvet box from his jacket pocket and showed us the ring. It was a beautiful and romantic idea; I only wish I thought of it myself.

The next time I saw Alex she could not wait to tell me about the proposal. I tried to act surprised but of course she knew that I was already consulted in the decision. "It was a beautiful proposal," she went on, "he took me on a boat across the river Thames and then when we came back, we went to a beautiful restaurant. I forget the name. Ah, it was Simpson's in the Strand, have you been?"
"I haven't but Claudia's brother Joseph is the head chef there,"
"Isn't it just wonderful Sam! I am to be married! He said that he can move both myself and Hanna the day before the wedding, into his uncle's property! Or I should say his property now, and he said we'd go for our honeymoon in Venice, I can't believe it! I am so excited"
"I am so happy for you Alex; you truly deserve everything this man can provide for you"
"Thank you." she blushed modestly "How is Claudia doing?"
"So much better since you spoke to her. I was shocked to see the change, but it was a welcomed relief"
"I can only imagine. The poor woman was heartbroken, I am surprised I was able to pull her out of her misery."
"We both are truly grateful for its Alex... anyway how is Hanna? Has she accepted Andrew yet?" "She loves him, don't get me wrong I don't think she is fully aware all the time as to who he is or why he is around so often, but he is kind to her, and she has taken to him well."
"I am so pleased for the both of you, it seems things are finally working themselves out."
"It's about time" she joked, and we enjoyed the rest of

our lunch as Alex spoke about her plans for the wedding.

For the second time that year Claudia and I attended a beautiful wedding. This time the room was filled but only with Andrew's family and the few friends Alex had. It was held in the winter of 1910 and they used the season as inspiration for the decoration of the hall that all the guests attended after the ceremony in the church. Alex was always artistic and although she had lost her passion for it after moving out with Hanna, I could see she found it again. Alex's wedding was very much like my own in terms of attendees. No family but Hanna and I and only friends to make up the absence. She seemed too distracted with her happiness to be concerned with this fact, but I could see through the smile, she was hurt that her life had turned out like this, and it shouldn't have, she didn't deserve it. But I ignored this to help her forget about it and we all had a great day. Claudia and I left a little earlier than most on the evening of the wedding which may have seen rude to most, and in fact we did have a few stares from Andrew's family, but nonetheless we decided to go home and we would not be pleasant company if we stayed. It was really Claudia who wanted to leave so soon, and as much as I wanted to stay for my sister, I could not let Claudia travel home alone. I made my way through the crowd of guests to give my final congratulations to Alex and say goodbye, "I am so sorry Alex, but Claudia has taken ill and she wishes to go home and rest" Alex gave me a sly grin and then glanced at Claudia, "I understand, please don't worry about leaving so early, I understand whole heartedly." I was confused and concerned about her reaction, but I did not question it as I did not want to leave Claudia waiting. "Well I'll see when you get back from Venice. Congratulations" I said and we hugged briefly before she let me go.

When we returned home, Claudia appeared to have had a sudden improvement in health, and instead of going straight to bed, as she said she was going to at the wedding, she sat in the sitting-room and asked me to make us some tea. "Claudia? what's happened? Did you have a problem with someone in the wedding? Is that the real reason you wanted to leave so early?"
"No not at all but I have some exciting news I wish to tell you, and it just so happens to be the reason I was feeling sick earlier. But first make us some tea and join me on the couch." I obeyed. When I returned, I found my wife blooming with life, a smile that I had not seen since our wedding day had taken residence in her face. Once I sat down, I gave her, her cup of tea and put my own on the table as it was of course boiling, she imitated then gave me the best news of my whole life. "Sam, I wanted to wait until I was absolutely sure, so I went to the doctors yesterday with Alex and he told me my suspicions were true. I'm pregnant!" she rejoiced; I could not speak. Happiness filled me from head to toe and my immediate reaction was to hold Claudia as tightly as I could. She cried tears of joy in my arms and we spent the next few moments like this. Alex's reaction had made sense now and once again two of the most important women in my life made me proud to be acquainted with them. We wanted to wait a little longer before we told anyone else about our unborn child, partly because we wanted to make sure there would be no complications and because Mary was nearing the end of her own pregnancy. When we went to visit them in the hospital after the birth of their daughter, Margaret, we had no choice but to tell them as Claudia was showing and Mary immediately caught on.
"Congratulations!" Oliver said hugging us both, "I am so happy for both of you" said Mary, but of course she

couldn't get up as she had just had a baby and was cradling her in her arms. "Thank you" I replied, "it is exciting isn't it, our children will be near enough in age that they can grow up together," Claudia said addressing Mary who began to cry at the thought, Oliver and I could do nothing but laugh at the two. Once Alex had returned from her honeymoon in Venice and had settled into her new home, we invited her, Oliver, and Mary to help us with the nursery. During this process I was reminded endlessly of when Hanna was born and how Claire and her mum had to decorate the nursery themselves because our dad was AWOL and our mother was dead. I wondered if Alex thought about this too, if she did, she never let on.

CHAPTER TWELVE

It was the 12th of December 1910 when our son was born. The night was wild and as cold as that winter had been up to this point. I stayed with Claudia as our son ripped his way through her, throwing her into agony and all for his selfish intentions of living. The smell of blood drifted past my nose like it was taunting me and made me nauseous, but I could not leave. I had to be there to save her if this child tried to take her from me. It felt like hours before the torment was finally over. The screams of my poor wife still haunt me as I write this. I felt intense guilt for standing by as she went through so much pain, but what could I have done. When the nightmare was over, we were introduced to our new-born baby boy. It was strange to see such a beautiful, innocent being come from such a painful and violent affair. There is no love that can compare to that of a father and his son, but more so for a mother and her child. When I saw this boy, I knew that all my life would be dedicated to protecting this being that I created with my love. The first time I held him felt like magic, a connection that I had never felt before came over me so sudden that I thought I would shed a tear.
"Isn't he just beautiful Sam? That is our son"
"I don't think I'll ever feel this way about anything other than our child Claudia, you should be so proud.

You were so brave."

"There is no room for pride in myself when I have a child so perfect and innocent as this little man" Claudia handed him over to me and I rocked him gently to sleep, "What shall we call him?" she asked me, "I am not sure, do you have any ideas" I replied "I was thinking about Bartholomew, which means his name would be Bart... like your father"

"Claudia... I – I think that's a wonderful idea, what made you come up with that?"

"I know you didn't get along with him in the end, but in the beginning, it sounded like he wasn't a bad man and maybe we can change the past with this little one"

"I love it." I whispered swallowing the lump in my throat. It is true that near the end of his life I did not like my father very much. But as much as I resented him, I could not help but sympathise with the man. He sacrificed everything to give his family the best life he could, and then he lost his wife. His reaction to such a loss was extreme and I do not approve of his behaviour towards us and Claire by any means. Nonetheless we all react differently to grief, and although we lost our mother, he lost his wife.

My parents grew up together in Prussia. Their own families lived next door to one another in a wealthy part of Prussia where everyone's estate was large. It was a very populated area which meant everyone knew everyone but not everyone cared much for their neighbours. However, my grandparents were friendly and loved to socialise, so they got on with their neighbours well. This is how my parents met. Before they were born their parents decided to build a door in the wall that separated the gardens so they could come and go as they please and it would have been easier for their children, when they came to play together. So, by the time my dad was born the two couples were as thick as thieves thanks to this renovation. My mother was born a couple of months after my dad. He was a winter child and my mum were a spring. The two became close quickly and since my dad's parents already had my uncle Oskar, my mum's parents spent a lot of time with them making sure they were doing the right thing but also relating to one another with their experiences. It was also a benefit in terms of child-minding because by the time they were both five they ended up sharing one nanny. According to my mother they never had a problem with sharing toys because if she ever wanted one my father had he'd give it up to her immediately and it was the same story if they were playing games in the garden. My dad treated my mum like she was the queen in his life and didn't stop until we moved to England.

By the time they were twelve there was a joke that had spread among all the other children in the neighbourhood about them one day getting married. This joke spread so far that their own parents joined in. My dad started going to work with his own dad to earn some money, his dad was a lawyer so he couldn't do much but file and organize, but he earned a respectable wage for a twelve-year-old. With that money he took my mother out to cafe's and when they got older, they would go to the theatre, all of this was with a chaperone of course. On one of these days when they were fifteen years old, my dad told my mum that one day he wanted to marry her. My mum at the end of the day immediately told my grandmother and immediately the two families pooled together to save for the wedding and their first house. Of course, they had their fights since they both were working towards demanding careers, but nothing could have broken them apart. As it happens when they moved to different towns almost two hours away from one another to study what they each wanted to study individually they still wrote frequently and in fact my mother let me keep one of the letters my dad had left her when they were both visiting their families for Christmas;

Dear Nadia,

I want to apologise for my behaviour over Christmas. I should never have accused you of favouring my brother over me especially after all we've been through together. Being apart from you has proven to be the biggest challenge of my life and I fear it has started to consume me in the worst way possible. I wish I could be with you rather than be here studying this nonsense, and I would leave and study anything else so I could be nearer to you, but you know my father would never allow such defiance.

The love I have for you may be the death of me one day, but I have no doubt it will be one that is peaceful, as there is nothing purer in the world than your existence. I hope you will write back to me once you have the chance.

Sincerely and full of love, Bartosz

Reading this letter now changes how I perceive my dad, and I see he was right about my mother being the death of him although it was not one close to peaceful, but instead filled with resentment, spite, and darkness.

After university they moved back in with their families and started working just outside of the wealthy neighbourhood. After the wedding they attained a manor in a neighbouring town, and there they grew their own family. I was born two years into their marriage and my sister four. For a while we were their proudest achievements. While we were still in Poland my mother worked part time so she could spend as much time with us as possible. At the time my father loved the idea, for at this time they were comfortable in wealth and my mother did not need to work as much as she did in England. I remember little from my time in Prussia, but I do remember my mother taking us to the park and occasionally to our grandparents' estates. I remember loving to run around and play pretend games with myself in my grandparent's gardens, and as young as I was, I was able to make a couple of close friends with the other lads in the park. It is fair to say that Poland was the best place for our family to be. When my father came home from his work, and now he always came home as early as possible to either help with dinner or have a family dinner. He wanted to spend every moment he could with his wife and young children. He felt an incredible sense of pride to have his family and the only reason that changed was because of the transition between Poland and England. So, you see why I sympathise with my father despite his actions, because as I have said, we lost our mother, but he lost his wife.

Watching my son grow was a unique experience. One blink and he was no longer a new-born another and he learned how to walk and another he was speaking full sentences. It seemed like no time at all until he was a toddler. I tried to take as much time as I could away from work to be with him, but I found it near impossible due to my new financial responsibility, children are expensive and unfortunately, I learned that a bit too late. Claudia, on the other hand, had left her job at the cafe. It took a little bit of encouragement but after she saw his face, she knew she couldn't bear to spend a second away from Bart. Although it put more pressure on myself to bring in the money that we were now missing out on and I wasn't able to see Alex as much, not that she had much free time herself as she refused to allow Andrew to hire staff for their new estate. But it was worth it when I came home every day to my family. I won't lie it wasn't easy in the beginning as Claudia and I were getting acquainted with our new routine, but we worked our way through it. One of our hardest arguments was when I had to do overtime and I came home tired and lacking any ounce of patience I had left, "you're late." Claudia stated flatly, I tried to be as calm as possible "Alton asked me to stay and work a bit later,"

"did you not think of the fact you have a son at home? And that maybe your wife was struggling to put your son to bed?" I couldn't hold on to the lack of respect and gratitude I was being shown so I bit back, "I did think of my family, and when I considered the overtime I thought that if I did it my family might be able to have a bit extra money for a day out at the end of the month,"

"excuse me? You were the who convinced me to stop working at the cafe, don't you dare act like it's my fault we don't have as much money as we used to have"

"I never did such a thing!"

"Don't shout, I've spent an hour trying to get Bart to sleep," I saw then her exhaustion and I tried to comfort her, "you are doing a wonderful thing by taking time off to raise our son, I appreciate it greatly. But maybe you should take him over to see Mary and Margaret during the day. I'm sure the two could give each other a break and maybe split the workload?"

"Are you saying I can't look after my own child myself?" she responded defensively, "not at all, you said you were overwhelmed, and I gave you a solution." she stormed off without saying a word more and we stayed in two separate rooms that night. In the morning before I went to work, however, I wrote her an apology note and when I came back from work, I brought her a bouquet, and all was well once again.

CHAPTER THIRTEEN

It was on June 28th, 1914, a day I think the whole of England will remember if they were old enough. The broadcaster broke the news of the Archduke's, Franz Ferdinand of Austria, assassination in the capital of Bosnia. The reporter said the motive of the murderer was political, but to Oliver and me this event, although tragic, was irrelevant to us. If only we knew what we know now, we may have prepared for the outcome. Although Oliver and I thought nothing of the news, the woman heard the word political and panicked, the next thing we knew, Mary and Claudia were bursting into the living room from the kitchen in panic, "Didn't you hear the news? That man that was assassinated, they say it was politically driven. Doesn't that put us in danger?" asked Mary in such an anxious fury, Oliver answered her, "Nonsense Mary, don't get yourself worked up over nothing"
"Why would they be telling us about something on the *British* news that has no effect on us?" asked Claudia, Oliver replied once again but this time making the ladies quite displeased with him, seeing their tempers rise after his first response I thought it smarter to stay out of it. "You women do get hyped up over nothing" he dismissed and looked to me for support, "It doesn't affect us at all, but some people may be interested in

international politics." I added trying to ease the tension in the women, "How dare you be so disrespectful! We were only asking a simple question that was deserving of a simple answer" Claudia demanded, "A simple question deserves to be asked calmly," Oliver responded naively, they stormed out of the room. Oliver and I looked at each other and laughed. "You're not wrong Oliver they do get hyped up over nothing" we laughed harder but quiet so we would not insult the women more and ultimately make the situation worse for ourselves. "Anyway, Sam we should get going, it will be Margaret's dinner time soon and Mary will be dying to give me an earful when we are home."

"Very well, it was nice seeing you both and Margaret, she is getting so big and beautiful, you can tell she will be just like her mother when she is older,"

"Well god forbid she is ever like me" he joked "But thank you Sam, shall we expect you both for dinner this Sunday?"

"Of course, are Nolan and Rylan still joining us?"

"As far as we are aware, but you know what they're like, they cancel every time, Cromwell's resorted to not inviting them altogether, I don't think he's invited them to Christmas dinner. But either way it will be a good night if they don't."

"Of course, and give Aileen and Brandon my love, I haven't seen them in a while,"

"Neither have I. It's the old age you know? it can get to you"

"Ah yes," I laughed, "well I do hope they're doing well"

"I'll let them know that you are asking for them. Mary we should probably get going so Margaret can get her tea." Mary and Claudia had said their goodbyes and as soon as they had left Claudia become cold towards me. "What did I do?"

"You know what you did"

"It was not me who said anything it was Oliver"
"And you let him"
"He is in a way right, you women do get yourselves in such a state over nothing" she gave me the deadliest stare but all I could see was her kindness and her gentle and good nature, so it felt like I was getting scolded by a child and I could not help but laugh a little. "What's funny?"
"I am so sorry it's just so hard to take you serious when you look so beautiful" I provoked a smile she tried hard to hide but couldn't. We joked together and the coldness had shattered, so I helped her with the dinner while Bart played quietly in the kitchen with us.

During the week while I was at work, I had discovered that it wasn't just the women that were concerned about the outcome of the assassination. I heard whispers from my colleagues about the news and that Sunday I discovered Oliver had a similar experience when we went for dinner. We were sitting in his sitting-room discussing the strange events of the week, "The chat in my firm was relentless about this assassination," he said, "It was the same in my own office, it seems the whole country has gone mad." I replied, "I saw my father during the week and all he did was mutter on about war."
"War! Absurd. It won't amount to that"
"My thoughts exactly. Mary was convinced for a bit of the same outcome, but I managed to sway her once I told her that the reason Margaret wasn't sleeping at night was because she wouldn't stop rattling on about the danger, we were all in,"
"What a shame. They should really be considering the audiences before they go blurting such news that now has the entire of London in a panic,"
"I could not agree with you more Sam. But there is something I need to tell you that is not relevant to this

whole war nonsense."

"What is it? You look like you've just spotted death in the corner of the room"

"It's my mum Sam, she has taken ill. When I went to see my dad, I noticed she wasn't there and when I asked my dad about it, he said she had some sort of attack and was rushed into the hospital on Monday,"

"What hospital was she taken to?"

"well the Lewes Victoria hospital of course," as much as I felt my own grief and fear for Aileen, especially since she was in what I considered at the time and still do now in fact, a cursed hospital, I thought Oliver had more right to express his as it was his mother, "What can I do for you Oliver? It is a difficult thing to be losing your mother, but at least she may have hope left"

"I don't think there is anything you can do for me, but I do think you should come and see her with me this Thursday. I know she would greatly appreciate it."

"Of course, shall we travel first thing in the morning?"

"I think that would be best." he replied flatly. I won't lie I didn't want to see Aileen simply because I knew she wasn't going to live for as long as she stayed in this hospital, but I saw Aileen as my mother so I knew if I didn't say my final goodbyes it would be a regret that would follow me on for the rest of my life.

The next morning, I got up early, not that I slept much. I didn't want to wake Claudia or Bart as it was so early, so I walked about the house as quiet as a ghost. "What are you doing up so early?" Claudia had said while standing in the kitchen doorway, "I told you Oliver and I were going to see Aileen today,"

"Not this early. It's six o'clock,"

"I couldn't sleep any longer so I thought I'd make some tea," she walked over to me and took the kettle from my hand, "here, go sit down, I'll sort the tea," she said and I obeyed. When she brought the tea through she

had made one for herself, "you should go back to bed," I told her, "nonsense, Bart will be up in no more than hour, at least now I can have a cup of tea before I have to get him ready for the day," I smiled at her, but couldn't stand her gaze so I looked back down at my tea. "You're allowed to grieve Sam. She was like a mother to you; anyone would expect you to be devastated." "I've already lost my mum and Oliver was there for me, so I have to do the same for him," she shook her head but dropped the subject. Just as Bart woke up it was time for me to go, so I kissed them both goodbye and headed across to Oliver's house. He didn't look like he was grieving although he said himself that Aileen didn't have much of a fighting chance, "alright Sam," he greeted me cheerfully, I wasn't sure how to react, but to be on the safe side I tried to match his enthusiasm, "alright Oliver, you ready to go?"
"aye, Mary and Margaret are still in bed, I'll just go say bye to them and we can be off." he ran upstairs and was back down within seconds and then we were off.

Walking up those hospital stairs once again felt like a job in itself. I was so tired of seeing this hospital, so sick of its white walls and the smiling nurses. When I saw Aileen, she seemed so weak and frail that the image of her shocked me so much my heart jumped. I was looking at true death when I saw her. Throughout her life she was so lively and happy, and now all she was a porcelain doll, cracked and withered, and ready to be taken away. When she saw us, she smiled a beautiful and bright smile that brought some of the life back into her empty face. I was so pleased to see her illness did not kill her spirits. "My boys!" she said and beckoned us forward with wide, frail arms. "How are you Sam?"
"I'm doing fine, but more importantly, how are you?"
"Do you see where I am? I'm not doing too well" she

laughed "That was a silly question now I think of it" we were interrupted by a nurse, "Oh! I see you have visitors Aileen, is this your boys?"

"Yes, this is Oliver, and this is Sam"

"You must be pleased to have some visitors today." the nurse turned to us with a disapproving look,

"I am indeed," Aileen seemed cold towards this nurse and I was eager to know why but I thought I had a good idea why. When she left, I didn't have to ask before she came out with the reason on her own. "That woman thinks I'm a child, did you hear her there, 'how are you today Aileen?' how do you think I bloody am?" we could not help but laugh at her forwardness, especially because the nurse had only left the room seconds before she went on about her. She looked at Oliver, "How is your father?"

"I haven't seen him today yet; I came straight here to you"

"You will go see him soon though, won't you? I don't think the house will be standing if he's left to fend for himself for too long" we both laughed with her, but I sensed a slight bit of seriousness in her voice. "It won't be long until you're out anyway and you can go back and keep him company yourself" she looked at Oliver gravely and his expression dropped, "Has the doctor changed his mind? Does he think you're getting worse?" he blurted "Now Oliver don't play a fool, I raised you better than that"

"What do you mean? Are you not getting better?" I chimed in, "Look at me, both of you. I'm old, if this illness doesn't take me the age will, but let's not lie to ourselves as to which is more probable"

"Mum that is absurdity and morbid. How could you be thinking like this? what about Margaret?" "My love for my family is not enough to beat the inevitability of death, Oliver."

"I will not hear anymore," Oliver stood up in rage,

"You have given up before the battle has been fought!"
"When you get to my age you will understand yourself" she stated as Oliver stormed out of the room like a stubborn child while I sat in shock, "Sam, you have always been a good friend to him." she began, "You have seen more death than he has, you will understand better. Could you please look after him for me? And make sure he looks after his dad. I would ask my older two, but they are all the way at the other side of the country." she took my hand and I saw tears build up in her eyes. "I have seen more death than Oliver," I said, "which pains me to this day, but none causes me more grief than that of your fatal end, please let me make you that promise that you have asked of me and this time I will keep it. I promise to look after your son and my friend Oliver, and I promise to make sure he stays close with his dad and siblings. There is something that I have neglected telling those in my life who have passed, but I will not allow myself to leave this room without thanking you. You took in a boy who was nothing but your son's friend and for that I am forever grateful. I hope to make you proud."
"Samuel, you are more than my son's friend, we may not be blood, but I see you as one of my own. Tell me, do you believe in heaven and hell?"
"Honestly, I'm not sure, when my mother died, I did, but now I- I don't think I can," she squeezed my hand and then pulled me close to her. We sat in each other's arms for a few moments and then I pulled away, "I will send Oliver in,"
"Thank you" she said through tears.

Oliver stood out in the hall; he was also crying. "Oliver," I said as I attempted to comfort him, he gripped on to me tightly, I knew how he felt. I knew how alone and helpless grief made him, even though he was an adult I knew the pain that came with losing a mother, losing the woman who is supposed to keep you safe from any danger. A mother to a child is a saviour, an angel sent from heaven, your own guardian who would fight away all evil when you were vulnerable. And to have that ripped away from you regardless of your age is so painful that it can sink you into the darkest of places. "She's dying Sam. I'm losing my mum,"

"You should see her once more Oliver, I guarantee you will regret it if you don't" he pulled away wiped his face and straightened himself, "You are right," he went back into the room as I waited in the hall. I thought they would respect their privacy at this time. She was a wonderful woman, and as I said before if you met her you would have felt lucky. There was a sort of injustice I felt when being told of her illness, it made me question the existence of god as I couldn't understand why he would take such an amazing woman from us. I didn't understand this feeling at all or why it made me question so much of the world and religion. I don't mean to seem impolite, but the woman was nowhere near her youth anymore, she is nearing the golden years of eighty and it showed a little more than she would have hoped for. Nonetheless she lived to see her last two children grow and get careers they desired in their later youth and she lived to see three of her grandchildren. She lived to give them the great memories that she gave all her children, including me, the boy that she took in out of no obligation, and made him her son. So why I felt so much grief I did not know. Her life was full of joy and kindness, and she will leave a legacy behind her that is greater than a king's.

Near the end Oliver had moved in with his dad which meant he could visit Aileen as often as possible so she wouldn't be alone. During the time he was away Claudia and I hosted Mary and Margaret to help support Mary in his absence, the children loved it since they didn't fully understand what was happening around them and the grief, we were all experiencing. In the following week after we saw her, she had passed. Oliver said she was sleeping, but he knew when it happened. We had offered to keep him as well until after the funeral and thankfully he and his family did stay. Oliver kept himself busy with planning Aileen's burial while he was with us but after that he turned into a hermit and we didn't see him for a while. Mary said he had cracked and was paranoid over the least little thing in terms of their health. According to Mary when Margaret had a cold, he rushed her to the hospital and more or less forced the doctors to do every test they could to make sure she wasn't sick. Soon enough he forbids Mary and Margaret to go out if it was raining or cold or if there was any illness going about that they could catch. For a month we were communicating through letters which was nonsense since we lived just across the road, but he was so paranoid of interacting with us in case we had an illness, or they had an illness that had gone undetected. If we had run into one another in the shop, he would cover his mouth with his scarf and try to convince me to do the same. The man had lost his mind. But it was when he himself stopped writing those letters that I decided I was done and went to break him out of his paranoid condition.

When the first letter came in that was signed by Mary I immediately put on my coat and went across to his house. It was Mary who answered the door, "Oh thank goodness," she rejoiced, "can you please talk to Oliver he hasn't left his study in three weeks,"
"Three weeks? Has he gone mad?"
"I fear he has; he won't let us near him either, he says he could be contracting something contagious, but I don't see how as he hasn't left the house since he last

went into his study."

"this is all nonsense, I will not leave until he has come to his senses," Mary opened the door wider and let me in, "thank you Sam" she said filled with sincerity. I walked in to see him scribbling furiously on single sheets of paper, he did not look up to see that it was me, "Mary I told you I am terribly busy, I cannot be distracted."

"It's me, Oliver"

"Sam! What on earth are you doing here? Is Claudia and Bart alright?"

"They are fine Oliver it is you who I am concerned for. What are you writing?"

"My will, I have to make sure all of my savings are split between, Mary, Margaret and my Dad. But why are you worried about me?"

"Your behaviour, Oliver, is concerning, Mary told me you haven't left your study in three weeks! And you're a perfectly healthy man writing his will."

"This world is dangerous. Anything can happen to them, there are so many evils that I cannot protect them from and if I'm gone, they will need my money. There is no harm in being prepared, you always were."

"Not for someone to die Oliver! That is absurd. You've been in this room for three weeks, Margaret has probably forgotten what you look like and Mary is ready to send you to the asylum," when I mentioned his daughter I seemed to have gotten through to him, he looked up at me and for the first time since I had entered it seemed he was listening, "Oh no, I had forgotten all about Margaret," he broke down into tears as I walked over to his desk to comfort him, "maybe you need a break Oliver. Perhaps if you go to your dad's for a little while you'll start to feel more like yourself." he stood up, "you're right, but I have to talk to Mary about it first and I should apologise to her," he walked to the door and downstairs, I followed him and was pleased to see he hugged Mary and apologised to her. Believing my job was done I left and went back home. When Oliver did eventually go see his dad, he went alone. I expected that this was Mary's idea and I can't say I blamed her. At what was supposed to be the end of his trip he prolonged it from a week, to two then two to three and then it became two months before he returned, and what convinced him that he couldn't wait a second longer I will come to in a moment. However, I must bring this story back to my sisters.

After Aileen had passed, I wrote to Alex informing her of the loss, although it did not affect her as much as it did Oliver, she was still acquainted with Aileen and on many occasions, Aileen would extend her kindness to Alex. She wrote back to me asking me to give Oliver her sincere sympathy for his loss and then asked if we could meet. We arranged a lunch in our usual restaurant the next again week and it was here that I learned the disturbing truth of Hanna's condition. "I'm so sorry to hear about Aileen, I know you were close," she said as we sat down at the table, "Thank you, but it is Oliver who is experiencing a great deal more of the grief. He's had to take some time apart from us all and he has went to stay with his dad," she looked at me puzzled, "It was for the best, he needs the change of scenery and we all thought that spending some time with his dad would be a good thing, but anyway, how's Hanna doing?" I asked, and my question was met with an expression filled with shame. "I must confess Sam; I may have been a little naïve to my ability when it has come to Hanna's care. There was one-night Andrew and I were asleep and Hanna, as far as we were aware was also asleep, but I had awoken suddenly as I felt something was wrong. I opened my eyes and saw legs in front of me, bare legs, and as I looked up it was Hanna standing over me stark naked. I got such a fright but I did not

want to wake Andrew so I gently got up and took her through to the hall, but Sam..." she began to cry softly, "as we got into the light she was covered in her own blood." the last part she whispered as of course she did not want to start any rumours. "Alex, what on earth was she doing?"
"I can't tell you, but it took me so long to scrub her clean, it was like she had stood there like that for hours and the blood dried so hard into her skin. But that is not my only worry. I did not want to tell you like this but, I'm expecting, and although I should be happy, I am worried about Hanna being around the baby. I haven't told Andrew yet because I'm not sure what to do,"
"This is wonderful news Alex, but I understand the turmoil that surrounds it as well." I began, struggling with what to say next, "I am so sorry I can't take her in myself because we have Bart but... I want you to be opened minded with what I am about to suggest-"
"No! We cannot put her away like some animal!"
"We aren't doing that at all, all we're doing is finding a better form of care for her so we can all live better lives. Including Hanna,"
"She's not mad"
"No one is suggesting that, but you can't take care of Hanna when you have a child on the way. It's far too dangerous,"
"But she can't be thrown into a cage and treated like a wild and dangerous creature either. Is there not family in Prussia that we have?"
"No. Mother was an only child and father hated his older brother. Don't remember how they spoke of him when we moved to England? And Alex they don't keep them in cages if they're not criminals but if you wait any longer you run the risk of Hanna becoming exactly that," she looked down in shame, "how about we both talk to Andrew about it and see what he says. After all it's his child as well and he has a right to have say in

what happens to it." she could only nod, so I did not press her further on the subject.

Andrew was working late that evening, but I assured Alex I could wait. When entering Alex and Andrew's estate it was completely silent, for the first few moments I feared that Hanna was dead but seeing how calm Alex was, I realised this was how it always is. "would you like some tea?" she asked as we entered into a large sitting-room decorated in red tapestry and mahogany furniture. When Andrew said the estate was nice inside as well, I didn't doubt him, but I didn't think it would look this grand. "I would love some tea," I finally replied after getting over my shock and I took a seat on the expensive looking couch as Alex disappeared into the kitchen. She came back shortly after with the tea tray. "Where is she?" I began, "you couldn't have left her here alone,"
"I didn't. She's with the nurse upstairs,"
"Oh, so you did take my advice and get Hanna professional care" I realised it sounded like I was rubbing it in after she looked at me with a deadly stare, "no, I didn't mean it like that. I mean you could hire the nurse full time and move her in, surely there's enough room for that" I said excitedly but she looked down to her tea and began to cry, "what's the matter?" I asked, "the nurse did move in with us a month ago," I think then we both realised the gravity of the situation. I sat my tea down and moved closer to my sister and gave her comfort by putting my arm around her, "I'm so sorry," she cried harder and then sat her own tea down and threw her hands around my neck. She must have cried an hour before she managed to pull herself together, but I didn't mind, she needed someone in that moment to care for her like she did for everyone else. "Shall I get her?" she asked me drying her eyes, "if that's alright," I replied "I would love to see her," she

left the room and went upstairs, a few minutes later I was joined by Hanna who was now sixteen years old and her nurse, Miss Audrey Marston, "Mrs Melvin has just gone to wash her face she said she'll be done in a moment," the nurse said politely, "thank you" I replied and then turned to Hanna who was staring at me although she didn't seem like she was seeing me, "hi Hanna, do you remember me?"
"I'm sorry to interrupt sir, but Hanna sometimes forgets who I and Mrs Melvin are, so please forgive her if she doesn't" nurse Marston added, I nodded to her but before I could say anything else Hanna came close to my face and expressed some form of recognition. I took her hand, "it's Sam, Hanna, it's your brother" I said quietly, she didn't seem to acknowledge anything I said and instead abruptly ran to the kitchen, the nurse ran after her. Alex had resurfaced shortly after and in enough time to hear the chaos in the kitchen created by Hanna. "I usually tell Audrey to keep her in her room," she said languidly.

It was late before Andrew got home and Alex was falling asleep. I wanted to wait as I didn't trust she would tell Andrew the truth. However as soon as he got home and saw me sitting on the couch he knew something was wrong, "what's happened?" he asked in a panic, I looked at Alex who didn't move but looked at him when he spoke, she began to cry again but managed to force out the words, "Hanna is very ill, Sam thinks I should send her away,"
"Tell him the whole story Alex," I demanded, "I'm having our child and Hanna is getting worse and worse. It could be a risk keeping a child here where she is" he looked between us both in shock and confusion, "I don't think I understand," he finally said, "Hanna is beginning to do strange things that one would have to be mad to. If she continues to stay here it could be fatal

to the child." I stated and he seemed then to know what his only option was. When I went home that night, I knew Claudia would be furious and just as I expected she was waiting for me sitting on the stairs. As I entered the house she gave me a grave expression, "where were you?" she asked severely, I sighed remembering the stress I had just dealt with, "I was with Alex, she's pregnant" I said flatly, her entire demeanour changed, "well that's wonderful, isn't it? Why do you look so grim?"
"Hanna's condition is getting worse and – well, we're having to send her to the asylum to protect the child and herself," Claudia stood up and hugged me, "I'm sorry, how about a cup of tea,"
"I would love one,"
"go sit down and I'll meet you in the sitting-room," I did as she said, and we spent the night talking about how her day went.

When the time had come for Hanna to be taken to hospital, I could see that before we had left Alex was already having one of the worst days of her life. It seemed Hanna could sense what was about to happen and according to Andrew had spent the night before and all morning crying and having tantrums. Alex had released Audrey from her position the day before, so she was left to deal with it all on her own. It was a battle trying to get Hanna into the car and I could see Alex was about to give in to her and let her stay at home, but Andrew said he'd rather be shot than put his child in danger. Alex sat in the backseat with Hanna trying to calm her down while Andrew and I sat quietly trying not to interfere with what was happening. As Andrew pulled into the asylum gates Hanna got worse. She screamed her lungs out and refused to get out of the car and if anyone tried to force her out, she would get violent. Andrew had to recruit the help of the asylums nurses who were trained in how to handle the violent patience. Not long after he went in, he came back out followed by two tall and muscular men who pulled Hanna out of the car a little too violently. Alex screamed at them to stop but they threatened to take her as well if she didn't let them do their job. Andrew and I thought it best if she waited in the car and after what those two men told her she was more than happy too. However, when I went in, I was told that both Alex and I had to sign the paperwork for Hanna's admittance, so I went back out to the car and convinced her to come in with me. "Alex, they need both of our signatures or they won't be able to take her," I said trying to sound as sympathetic to her as possible, "well maybe that's a sign" she responded bluntly, "you can't be acting like this. You are punishing her by not allowing her a chance to get better and you're putting your child's life in danger!" she looked at me, tears filling her eyes, "very well," she walked slowly back into the hospital with me and signed the paperwork. They had already taken Hanna into a different room, so she didn't have to see her remaining family throwing her away to strangers. When we left Alex sat in the car crying her heart out, begging us to take her back and leave her with Hanna or at least change our minds so she can take her home. But that wasn't possible. I felt bad, of course I did. But what could I do? Hanna needed help and Alex couldn't anymore now she was carrying her own child. It was for the best. At least that's what I told myself.

CHAPTER FOURTEEN

It was the 28th July 1914. Only a month had passed since we had taken Hanna to the asylum and I hadn't spoken to Alex since. However, I was receiving frequent letters from Andrew who kept me up to date with her condition. The letter I received the week before this day he said she was coming to terms with Hanna's absence, but what was to come I have no doubt put hold on her full recovery. All of my family were in the sitting-room, Claudia sat with me on the couch reading Jane Austen, Bart sat of the floor with his toys, playing quietly and I sat contentedly listening to the radio. Then the news broke. "Britain is at war with Germany" the prime minister's voice had said through the radio. If I'm being honest, I don't think I remember the prime minister coming on the radio in the first place. Everything before this moment has become a blur and everything after this moment didn't feel real in the moment. We all sat silent and still, including Bart who was only four years old at the time. Claudia snapped her head toward me after a few moments of us sitting like this and Bart began balling. "What do we do now?" she begged and stood up to comfort Bart. I looked at them and wondered how I could protect them from this, but I knew there was no answer. Bart continued to cry and soon we were joined by another sobbing child and her family. Oliver had burst into the sitting-room followed by Mary, Margaret, and Brendan. "Did you hear the news?" Oliver asked, "Of course we heard the bloody news!" I responded impatiently threw myself of the couch. "I told you," Brendan said taking a seat, "I told you it would lead to war"

"We know dad that is all you have said since you came in."

"What will happen to the children?" Mary pleaded, "don't worry about that, I'm sure the government will have thought that through before they started a bloody war," Oliver replied, I went to Claudia, feeling more rational, "Claudia why don't you and Mary go have a cup of tea and take the children up to Bart's room to play?" she nodded and obeyed. Once they were settled Oliver and I took a seat and began to work-out a plan to keep our families safe. "London will be safe surly," Oliver began, "I don't see why it shouldn't be," I replied, "well we should keep them here, dad, you'll have to move in with Mary and me until it's over. It will be safer for you,"

"Nonsense, I'm not moving all the way out here. Me and your mum have lived in the house for over sixty years,"

"It doesn't matter now your life is at risk," Brendan looked pleadingly to his son, "my whole life is in that house,"

"We'll go back and get what you need, but you can't stay there, not the now at least,"

"He's right Brandon, I'm going to see if Alex and Andrew will come and stay with us as well. It might be over in a week, who knows" he nodded but looked like a stubborn child while he did so. "Right, that's that,"

"You two will have more to worry about than what's going on here anyway," added Brendan, "they'll be expecting you to sign up. Especially you Sam."

"What do you mean, especially Sam? He's an

Englishman"

"Doesn't matter if he has the accent and the manners, he's still Prussian to everyone else, and right now everyone who's not British will be an enemy."

"Claudia is Prussian as well; will she be in danger?"

"Not if you fight for this country. You need to show England that you are dedicated to defend it." I hung on to every word he said, but I struggled with what to do. Do I leave my family to fight for my country? Or do I stay and fight for them? It took me a while to realise there was no difference between fighting the front lines for England and fighting for them.

Brendan took a while to adapt to his new life in London. Although he didn't like living in the city, he did enjoy having company again and spending time with his granddaughter. I went to see Alex and Andrew the day after the news broke. When I knocked on the door it was a strange woman who answered, "hello?" she said confused, "I'm looking for Alex and Andrew?" I replied, "Mr Melvin has gone to train for the army and Mrs Melvin has asked not to be interrupted," I never expected this response, however knowing Alex was alone I felt much more determined to bring her back to London, "can you tell Alex it's her brother and she must come back with me to London, immediately" I demanded and the woman seeing my urgency let me in, "if you will wait here then Mr Nowak," she hurried away and returned with a message from Alex, "Mrs Melvin is not in a position to get up and leave and would appreciate if you would return to London without her,"

"I will not. Where is she?" I demanded once more making my way up the stairs the woman had just returned from, "please, sir, you mustn't disturb her," I pushed open the first door I had seen that had a sign in front of it that read "do not disturb" and inside was

Alex. She was writing at a desk filled with files but when I burst into the room she stopped and flounced from behind the desk to me, "what on earth do you think you're doing?" she demanded "I'm sorry miss I tried to stop him but-" the woman pleaded, "No need to apologise Bertha, I know very well what my brother is like. If you wouldn't mind, can you give us a moment?"

"yes miss" the woman left the room and Alex looked at me disapprovingly, "how dare you storm in here like you have the right!"

"Who is that woman?"

"Not that it's any of your business, but her name is Bertha, the maid, Andrew took her on before he left. Now leave!"

"Do you think you are safe here alone!"

"I'm not alone, Bertha and the cook is here with me,"

"Don't be stupid, Alex. You need to be with your family. Come back with me to London,"

"My family? You mean the one you locked away like a wild animal?"

"Hanna was ill, Alex, you know that, Andrew thought the same, we all agreed."

"You mean you two agreed! I was just to listen and obey, like a child."

"Enough of this nonsense Alex you are coming with me to London," I grabbed her arm and tried to take her back downstairs with me, but she wouldn't "I am not!" she pulled back her arm and stood defiant, "I will not allow you to dictate my life anymore, it is mine to do as I please with and if I no longer have Hanna to take care of then I will take back all of those years I missed picking up after everyone else's mistakes." I stood for a moment stunned. I had no idea how much pain she felt or how much my own failures affected her, "Alex, I- I don't know what to say."

"There is nothing to be said. You must leave me be,"

she began to cry, I approached her to comfort her, but she pushed me away, "Alex, please, you must come with me. If you won't do it for yourself think of the baby. Do you want to risk that child's life before it has the chance to live?" she shook her head and took a deep breath, "very well. I'll pack somethings and I'll meet you in London"
"No, I'll wait for you to pack, my car is outside we'll go together," she didn't look me in the eye but instead took another deep breath and called for Bertha to help her prepare her things.

Once Alex was settled, she made a point of treating me coldly but enjoying the company of Claudia, Bart and Oliver and his family when they were over. I didn't mind, as long as she was safe. Not much changed in terms of the daily routine except Oliver and I both had to pick up the slack at work since so many young men were dropping everything to go join the front lines. Slowly there were posters popping up everywhere you looked, begging the men of England to join the front lines, and what followed from this was men in their early thirty's, similar ages to Oliver and me, signing up themselves. In November, only four months after the news of the war broke, I had an unexpected visit from Alton, my boss who over the years had become a good friend. We were all in the sitting-room, I was listening to the radio as Bart tried reading a book next to me, a new habit he had taken up at this point in his life as he had seen all of the adults around him doing the same, and Alex and Claudia sat chatting away quietly on the couch opposite us. This was when Alton had knocked on the door, not knowing who it was I looked to the women and they looked at me and knowing then they weren't going to move, I got up and answered the door.
"Hello Sam," he said in his usual cheery tone and let himself in as he always did, he walked straight to the

sitting-room and greeted everyone, "hello ladies," he began addressing Alex and Claudia, then he knelt down and shook Bart's hand, "hello little man," he stood back up, "Sam, is there a chance we could talk in private,"
"Of course, we can go to the kitchen," I lead him through, "would you like some tea?"
"No thanks Sam, it's a quick visit unfortunately, there is something I need to ask you," this time he sounded a lot more serious, "well obviously you know that we've lost a lot of good employees to this war and I don't blame them of course they're doing what they think is right, but it's meant that I've had to make up for it and you have been a lot of help for me with that Sam, I would say you are one of the best employees I've had and a good friend."
"Is everything alright, Alton?"
"Of course, but, I'm hoping to sign up and I'm going to need someone to take my place as the manager for the paper and there's no better person for the job in my opinion than you," I sat speechless for a moment, feeling both honoured and nervous and doubting my ability to do the job justice, but only a fool would decline, "Alton I'm honoured," I managed to finally say, "you've earned it Sam, but there's one thing I ask, please don't sign up Sam, the paper won't survive without both of us," I laughed, "you're right, but Oliver and I both said we would rather stay to protect our family," he smiled "that's great Sam, thank you, I must be going though, I want to sign up before they close for the day,"
"Well thank you Alton, and good luck, I hope to see you back soon,"
"They say it will be over by next year, so I'll be expecting my job back when I return,"
"Of course, I'll see you next year then." When he left, I went and told Claudia and Alex about my promotion and for the first time in months Alex smiled at me. I

thought then that there was no way I could leave London as there was too much to make me stay.
I was convinced London was safe or I would have never let Alex stay with us there, it was the same story with Oliver moving Brendan in with them. However, on Christmas eve, 1914, an air raid had ripped the security from the town and threw it in our faces. Never have I been more grateful for the local's paranoia of a disaster, as it was this fear that provoked them to turn train stations into shelters. So, when that first bomb dropped, my priority was getting my family safely into there.

CHAPTER FIFTEEN

When the first bomb went off it felt like an earthquake. Without fully comprehending what had happened I shook Claudia who had heard the noise as well, "What's wrong? What was that?" she asked in a panic, "Quick! Wake Alex I will get Bart. We need to go to the train station." I responded frantically and jumped out of bed hardly managing to put my slippers on properly before I was in Bart's room and rushing him downstairs, it is surprising how logically a person can think when in a fatal situation. "Quick!" I screamed up at Claudia and Alex "Sam? What's happening?" I could hardly understand a word Alex said through Bart screaming in my ear from fear, but I could make a good guess, "A bomb has gone off. We need to get to the train station quick before they get to this side of London." I could not think of anything else but my family at this moment, Oliver never popped into my mind either, until we were safely in the train station and I saw Mary cradling Margaret in her arms. When I was running to the shelter with Bart clutched to my chest, I didn't have time to fully comprehend my surroundings, the only thing I made sure of was that Alex and Claudia were close behind by looking over my shoulder and calling on them. The closer we got to the train station the more people we saw helping their more vulnerable family members all in a panic. The smell of smoke had suffocated the air and the farther parts of London were lit up with fire. The train station in London was no more than a twenty-minute walk from our home, but when you are sprinting for your life that distance seems a lot shorter. Luckily, the bombs did not reach us before we were secured inside the underground station.

The train station was filled with families and the noises of the crying children. There were many volunteers standing in different areas handing out blankets, food, and water. I took a blanket from one of them for Bart and Claudia and Alex took water. Once we had reunited, I scoured the room for Oliver and his family. They lived only across the road, but I did not see them among the others who were running for their safety. "There's Mary and Margaret," Claudia pointed to the woman sitting on the ground holding her child's hand. She took Bart from my arms and ran towards her, feeling the relief from having the weight of a child on my chest Alex and I walked slower toward them. "What's going to happen?" she asked me, nearly whispering, "honestly, Alex, I'm not sure. I should never have made you come her, I'm sorry, I thought it was safe." She smiled at me, "it's fine Sam, you did what you thought was best, its commendable," once we met Mary and Claudia I could hear Oliver speaking to someone round the corner and he soon emerged with Brendan and a police officer, "Evening sir, everyone must have a tag, including the children." The policeman handed me four tags and I passed them out between Claudia, Alex, and my son who was now peacefully asleep once again in Claudia's arms, I took him back to allow Claudia to rest. Mary had made Margaret a bed of blankets that she brought with her and made a pillow out of the blanket they were given when they arrived, I wish I was that organized so my

son wouldn't have to suffer any further than he had that night, but thankfully Mary had offered her resources to Bart. "Would you like to put Bart down next to Margaret? They can share the blankets and that one you have there you can use as a pillow like we did." I looked to Claudia and she nodded "Thank you, Mary," I said to her and she sat him down as gentle as possible, he stirred a little as I stood back up which I was worried meant he was waking again, but he didn't. "So peaceful. I almost envy them." commented Mary, "I know," responded Claudia. We all sat in a circle around the children, as we discussed our current situation. "When did they come?" asked Alex, "I'm not sure, as soon as I heard what I assume was the first explosion I woke up Claudia,"
"there was two explosions Sam, Mary and I heard the first one but didn't know what it was and then when the second one went off, we grabbed Margaret and ran straight for here." After this brief conversation, another bomb went off, this time closer to the train station so we felt the earthquake once more.

Our silence in the train station was broken after the third explosion, when an elder lady had decided she finally had enough of this, "Why don't *you* do something about it?" she mocked Oliver and I, "Instead of sitting down here with all us, go and fight with the other men instead."
"Mum," the younger woman sitting next to her gently nudged her arm, "Don't talk to them like that, they're staying to protect their family" Mary responded defensively, "I'm so sorry, she's just a bit agitated," the daughter added, but Oliver had a different idea, "You know what Sam? She's right. I think we should sign up."
"Oliver, no!" protested Mary, "What use are we down here? We're men! All the other men in London have

gone to fight for their country," Oliver answered her sternly, "You're dads to two infant children." Claudia added almost pleading, "you're here to protect your family," I moved closer to her and took her hand, "Oliver's right Claudia. We'll come back, but none of us will be able to live if all of us don't play our parts in this."

"Please Sam! Bart is only a boy he will grow up without you-"

"Without seeing me, but I will write and when this is all over you can tell him his dad is a hero. They say it will only be a year,"

"Why must I tell him? Don't you plan on coming home and telling him yourself?" she began to cry, "Of course, I do. But it won't be as believable if I tell him myself" she laughed, I knew I was hurting her, but she understood. Mary, on the other hand, was not pleased, "Oliver you're not leaving our daughter here while you go fight someone else's war."

"It may be someone else's war, but they have left us to win it. And so, for the sake of my family I will do as they bid and come home to my family and country, as a hero." She shook her head and they sat together holding hands a for a while before she said, "promise you'll come back."

"I promise." was his response.

When the night was over, we were met by the destruction that was left. Very few had their homes still standing, our street was one that was taken down by the raids. "You could come and stay with me in Lewes?" suggested Brandon, a little bit too happy that now he had no choice but to return home, "dad that's so kind of you."

"It is Brendan, thank you, really"

"You can come and stay in my estate, if you like, Claudia?" asked Alex, "are you sure, I'm sure my mum and dad wouldn't mind hosting us,"

"It is no problem really we are family after all. And I would like the company,"

"Thank you," I looked down at Bart who looked wide eyed around him at the destruction, I sometimes wish I saw the war from a child's eyes just to understand what he was thinking that day. "Are you close to Brendan, Alex?" Mary asked, "I don't believe I have noticed, but nonetheless Lewes is a small town and it won't be a long journey for the children to be together again. The estates big enough for you all to come and stay?"

"Kind offer, but I'm missing my own house,"

"Sam, there's the recruiter, we better go." I kneeled down to Bart, "I have to go away for a while with Uncle Oliver, but mummy and aunty Mary and aunty Alex will be with you no matter what. Can you do me a favour?"

"What?" he said in the voice of childhood innocence, "will you look after mummy, aunty Mary, aunty Alex and Margaret and the baby for me? You're the man now of the house now." he nodded his head without fully understanding the situation, I kissed him on the forehead and held him as tightly as I could. Then I moved to Claudia, "I promise. I promise on my life that I will make it home to you. I have Alex's address I will write to you as often as I can. Please forgive me." she cried but nodded her head and kissed me. I held her for such a long time, but it didn't feel long enough. She said to me as I let go, "if you die out there-"

"Claudia please I won't let that happen,"

"No, but if you do, I'll kill you" she laughed through her tears and I laughed with her. That was the last time I spoke to her in person before Oliver and I headed to war.

The recruitment officer asked us some basic questions, such as our age and nationality, and if we had any health conditions, then we were weighed and measured. Both Oliver and I fit the criteria they were looking for and were made to recite an oath. With one hand on a bible and the other raised I said, "I, Samuel Nowak, do make Oath, that I will be faithful and bear true Allegiance to His Majesty King George the Fifth, His Heirs and Successors, and that I will, as in duty bound, honestly and faithfully defend His Majesty, His Heirs and Successors, in Person, Crown and Dignity, against all enemies, and will observe and obey all orders of His Majesty, His Heirs and Successors, and of the Generals and Officers set over me. So help me God." once Oliver repeated the same ritual we were sent to training in North Yorkshire. As I sat on the train, my mind started to wonder, and my potential death started to become clear to me. I couldn't show these men that I was panicking. How pathetic they would have thought me if I revealed how fearful I truly was. The front lines were no place for the weak and yet weak I was. While I held my fear deep inside my body, Oliver looked plagued with thought, he was completely unreachable. I endured three months of what they referred to as "basic training", I would hate to see what the next level was like. We pushed through strenuous physical training and we incessantly rehearsed marching and following commands trying to make each command an instinct. All of this wouldn't have proven to be so difficult if we didn't have the drill instructor's strident voice in our ears from half past five in the morning to eight o'clock at night, but training for war isn't supposed to be easy. The more difficult it is the stronger you become, not just physically but mentally as well.

Oliver and I, among some of the other trainees were sent to the trenches in France. There wasn't much news from there and once we saw the nightmare it was, we weren't surprised. Other than the soldiers telling their families they were okay, there was nothing to indicate this. A trench was a topless tunnel dug into the ground with sandbags and coils of barbed wire on top to prevent enemies from easily attacking. Weapons and other necessary equipment were never left unattended, there was coves dug into the walls of the trenches for sleeping and it wouldn't be unusual to see a rat or other pests. Major General Charles Hallewell had met us halfway into our narrow exploration of the trench, "Private McCarthy and Private Nowak?" he asked although it sounded more like a statement, "Yes sir," we answered in unison. He looked us up and down, "very well, I'm assuming you have some writing materials with you?" both Oliver and I pulled out our pocket sized notebooks and miniature pencils, "right, your schedule; 0500 Stand-to, 0530 rum ration, 0600 stand down, 0700 breakfast, 0800 clean sleeves, weapons and trench. Dinner is at noon after that you have the choice of sleep or down time, 1700 tea, 1800 stand-to, 1830 stand down and then you will be expected to help with the work, digging trenches, getting stores, patrol, etc. I will not repeat myself so if you've missed something you better get it from someone else, am I understood?"

"Yes sir," thanks to our training I managed to write down every word and it was then burned into my memory, so I didn't need the copy I had in my notebook, but it was always best to have a back-up. It was seven o'clock when we arrived at the trenches, it hadn't gotten dark yet, but the sun was starting to set. A lot of the men were hard at work with their duties and it was at this moment of reflection, we realised how many injured men there were. We hadn't had a moment to fully grasp what we were looking at, through the shock of seeing what the trenches were really like, but now that our minds had adjusted we saw all those men who appeared to be sleeping, or dead, that were missing

arms or legs or were covered in blood soaked bandages. After seeing this I turned to one of the other soldiers who was carrying a crate of supplies, "why are these injured men still here," his empty eyes looked at me puzzled, "ah, you're the new recruits," he began, "they get taken to one of the local hospitals at night, but the bodies get taken straight back home so their families can give them a proper burial," he replied in a friendly tone, as if the topic wasn't morbid and deserving of humanity, but I would soon learn that's just how war works, "anyway, I don't think you'll be expected to do much since you've arrived so late, but you should be prepared to wake up just as early in the morning as you would have in training. War never sleeps they say. I'm Private Ainsworth, but you can call me John," he moved the crate to underneath one arm and shook both mine and Oliver's hands, "I'm Oliver and this is Sam, we just came in from North Yorkshire,"
"I was trained there myself, but I'm originally from Liverpool. Joined up after we got the news that my brother was shot, broke my mother's heart, begged me not to come but, honour called,"
"It was the same with our wives," I added, "once the first air raid happened in London, we thought it was our duty to sign up ourselves, they thought differently"
"terrible thing that, happened on Christmas eve did it not?"
"aye, absolutely devastating. None of us expected it," Oliver replied, "you never do, but it's good to have you both, we always need new men here on the front lines. Come on I'll introduce you around. Well I better take this down first but we can do both on the way," John then led us down the way the Commander had come and began to introduce us to the other men along the way, "alright Peter, this is the new recruits, Sam and that's Oliver," we shook Peter's hand, he was an older man with a stern face but when he spoke he seemed a

lot more approachable, "alright boys,"
"they've just come from North Yorkshire,"
"that right? My son trained there, although I told him not to come. I tried to make it clear what kind of life we were living here, if you could call it that, didn't matter a bit to him,"
"My wife would never let our son follow in my footsteps and join the war, she barely let me out," Peter laughed, "my wife tried to talk him out of it but once he got to fourteen he had a mind of his own and would refuse to change it for anyone. He's eighteen now, how old's your boy?"
"He's four, he was just starting to learn to read before the air raid in London,"
"Horrible business that, I hope they haven't stayed, they say the country sides safer than big cities,"
"No, no, they moved in with my sister, her husband joined the navy,"
"Did he? You don't know where he was stationed do you?"
"No, Alex wasn't able to get his letters because I convinced her London was safe," I scoffed, "we all thought that, don't blame yourself," Peter replied, "what about you Oliver, do you have a family back home?"
"I do, a wife and a daughter, same age as Sam's son,"
"I wish my own boy was still that age, would have stopped him from joining the bloody war,"
"Well Peter, we better be going, got many more men to meet," John said, and we followed him down the trench again.

We were introduced to many different types of men, some seemed younger than the age limit to sign up, but when asked they said they were eighteen. Then we came across Alton, and I must say, he was not happy to see me. "Sam!" he shouted when he saw John, Oliver

and I approach, "what are you doing here? You were supposed to stay back home and look after the paper," "I know, but London was bombed,"
"Bombed! How's your family?"
"They're fine, they moved in with Alex to Lewes,"
"That's good, did you see the office before you left? Is it still standing?" I gave him a grave look, "a lot of destruction, Alton, I was surprised to see that anything had survived," he sat down and looked to the ground as if he were a child in a huff, "oh well, we'll have to build it back up again when we return," I nodded, "I'm so sorry Alton I know you worked hard to build it up," "Don't be sorry lad, people have lost more because of this war than I have." we left Alton and John continued to introduce us around. Once we had brief introductions with everyone, John had filled us in on the plan for the following morning, "the general's got a plan of attack that he will brief us on in the morning, it will be early, so you better sleep now," he pointed to two coves in the wall side by side, "that's the best you're going to get for a bed while you're here," he said, "thank you," Oliver replied, "what time will the briefing take place?" "I'm not too sure, but it will be early. Don't worry though, someone will come and get you both."

The briefing took place at 0430, half an hour before we were to attack. Major General Charles Hallewell stood on a pallet, giving us a motivational speech before we faced death. Some of the men were very vocal about their doubts, which shocked me as I could never imagine questioning an authority, let alone one with a gun, "you can do this or go home a deserter! Your choice!" he silenced the worries of the soldiers but did not put them to ease. As 0500 approached I realised I held my breath and released it last minute. We took our positions and braced ourselves for war.

CHAPTER SIXTEEN

I heard nothing but the beating of my own heart. It echoed inside my hollow body as I waited for the call to attack. I had Oliver beside me, who I don't believe I have ever seen so angry. He looked like he could burst into flames at any second, but I assume this was his way of preparing to accept the potential end of his life. I thought back to Aileen at the hospital and I wandered if he thought of her too. "When your old you'll understand" she said on her deathbed, but we understood then and we were only thirty-two. It felt like hours waiting for that signal to charge, and I should have been relieved, but I wasn't. I wanted to get it over with. If this was the day, I was going to die I wanted to do it now. The signal was given and all together over a thousand men had charged onto no man's land with the fury of a wild animal.

My first instinct was to hide, and I had to fight a powerful urge to turn back. Without stopping I looked for a place to take cover. There were many large metal pieces, firmly standing in the ground that I later discovered, after hiding behind one of those that they were pieces of tanks that were a victim of an explosion.

My whole body shivered as I leant against the cold metal and scoured my mind for what I had been taught. The loud explosions of gunfire prevented my thoughts and then there were the screams of dying men that proved an even bigger distraction. Smoke suffocated the air around me, but I couldn't bring myself to move. The General ran to the same cover point, but it was clear he wasn't hiding, "move Private!" he scolded, "Now!" I couldn't respond, my whole body was numb with fear. The General moved close to me and said aggressively, "if you don't move now, you'll be sent home as a deserter, do you know what happens to deserters?" I shook my head, "they're shot, so you can die a weak man or be remembered as a hero by your country and your family," I took a deep breath and decided I had no choice but to join the battle. To think about your own mortal danger in a scene like this makes you more like an animal than a human and all the other men on the field are animals too which made it so much easier to kill them. I never knew death had such a foul smell, it filled the field and mixed into the smell of the damp dirt and the smoke, in any other situation this would have made me nauseous, but I couldn't think about anything. My breath was taken away from me by the violence that I was a part of. I ran through the field as the bodies piled up all around me, if I was close enough to someone, I would stab them if not I would shoot. When faced with a situation such as this it's hard to explain how you feel because there is no room for emotion or comprehension. Looking back now I can say I felt fear, anger, grief, but overall, I was excited. The prospect of holding so much power over someone else's life thrilled me like nothing else. And it was the adrenaline that I got from that that allowed me to continue on shooting. When that faded, as it always does eventually, I came to terms with what I had just done, and when that comprehension froze me, I made eye contact with one of the enemies. He looked like a frightened rabbit in the glare of a fox, his eyes begged me to let him go while his body fidgeted with whether or not to kill me, maybe I looked at him the same way. However one of us had to make the first move, and all I could think about was Bart. The whole world went silent as he came to mind. So I shot him.

Shoot to kill they tell you, and that is exactly what I did. A shot to the chest. It was so clear; the blood flew from him like red rain and he screamed with his last breath. It didn't sound as I imagined, I thought it would have been more piercing, but instead he sounded as if he had only been winded, like he was hit with a football rather than a bullet. But as proud as I should have been, I couldn't be. Because although an enemy he was a man, and he could have very well been like me with a wife, a child, and a pregnant sister at home. A family. A life. A reason to be fighting. I didn't just kill one man I killed many. From this one man there could have been multiple generations that would have went on to tell his story, as I am now, but I took that away. I was truly conflicted with myself and my power in this moment. But I had no time to sit and ponder this internal discord when there was a was right beside me. After I killed him my first thought was to run back to the trenches. And although I feared the judgement of my fellow soldiers, more specifically what the General will do to me when he returned, but that was not as powerful as the feeling I had after killing this man. I didn't realise that there were men who had already returned to the trench, granted, most were injured and medics, but some had also retreated like me. I wasn't greeted with the same judgement I prepared myself for, but instead they spoke to me as if nothing had happened. I ran into John who had retreated only ten minutes before I did, "alright, Sam," he said sympathetically, "how's the war going for you?" another man joked, John reminded me of the names of the three soldiers he was sitting with, "do you remember these three? Andrew, Douglas and Peter," they all waved, I nodded in return but then left abruptly to sit on my own. I found a cove and wedged myself into it. I closed my eyes and tried to go back to the place I went that allowed me to stop drowning in guilt.

Once the battle was over, I heard the remaining soldiers return in celebration of a victory. The General had congratulated and thanked them for fighting with him but then reminded them that it wasn't over, and it wouldn't be long before they would have to do this again. Not long after the General had sat with me and told me, "I understand that feeling. The feeling you get after you kill a man. Do you know why I pushed you on the field to stop hiding like a coward?" I nodded like a child being scolded by their parent, "good, but here's the thing, you can't always run from it, you're here now and you will be here to the end unless your too weak, in which case you'll be dead, either on the field or back home do you understand? you have to fight this war, it was a choice for you to be here" I sat with my head low as he spoke, "Do you have a family back home?"
"I have a wife and a four-year-old son, and my sister is pregnant, her husband is in the navy." He shot me a grave look "do you know where he was stationed? Your sister's husband I mean,"
"I don't. Why?"
"Not important. Anyway, don't you want to go back and make your family proud? To go back and be a hero, a hero for Britain? Give your little boy someone to look up to. I know you're not from here, and I know the other boys don't respect you as much for that reason, so why don't you prove them wrong. Prove your just as much a Brit as the rest of us"

"How can you get over this guilt. It feels endless, like I'll drown in it"

"You have to dehumanize yourself first Samuel, only for the duration for the war. You can spend as long as you need here, I'll keep the boys out of your way as long as I can, but please Samuel, don't let them win, don't let our enemy win. Not just for our country, but for your little boy. What's his name?"

"Bart, it's short for Bartholomew, my wife chose it."

"That's the name of a real man. I hope Bart gets to learn that from his dad." he left me alone and I sat for the greater part of an hour in silence on my own before my mind bounced back to Oliver who I had still not seen. Instead of allowing myself to think about him I turned my thoughts to Bart as I pictured him safe in Lewes with his family, where I longed to be, but it wouldn't take me long to drift to sleep in which I was with them once again.

When I managed to pull my pathetic body from the cove and over to the other soldiers who were playing cards and making a lot of noise, I was relieved to see Oliver was with them. "He has risen," joked one of the soldiers, his name was Anthony, a young fellow, he had only just his sixteenth birthday before he signed up and was dumped in the trenches, although he told the recruiters he was eighteen and only admitted it was a lie when Oliver interrogated him. He would speak to you as if he were excited and felt his job here meant something, but you didn't have to look too close to see the fear in his eyes and the vulnerability in his smile. It was hard to forget he was just a boy when you looked at him, no matter how hard he tried to convince you he was a man. Oliver looked at him with a severe glare and then at me with a smile, he stood up and pulled over another chair between him and Anthony, "here Sam, come and sit with us, we're about to finish this

round, you can join in on the next one." Oliver said, "Aye, come join us, I'm about to mop the floor with these amateurs anyway," added Peter. When you looked at him next to the other men it was clear he was much older, he could have easily passed for the age of Brandon, but he never owned up to his real age. He seemed experienced with a gun and he always made it back unscathed after every battle. No matter how old he was it was clear he was a great advantage to our side. There was soldier who appeared closer to his age, but he preferred to spend his time off the battlefield with the younger men, specifically Oliver who he could relate to as they were both Scottish. I sat in the chair in between Anthony and Oliver and asked the latter, "how long have you been back, I didn't see you,"
"I came back with the General. I looked for you, but Charlie said you needed some rest and to leave you be," I nodded stiffly in response. I had never played any game of cards before, but I knew from the reactions of the rest of the table that Peter did in fact win. "Told you Sam, sure you want to play the next round?" he asked sarcastically, "I've never played before," I confessed, "we'll teach you," offered Oliver but before I could respond Peter added, "teach you to lose he means, swap seats with John, I'll teach you," everyone laughed and John and I swapped seats. The rest of the night was spent playing cards and I did win a couple rounds as well.

In the following weeks we had several battles and each one became easier and easier, just like the General said. I realised that to dehumanise wasn't a conscious effort but one that came naturally after a few battles. I hate to admit it, but I became rather talented with a rifle and tactical as well. The General praised me in front of the rest of the soldiers after we had returned from the field, "good work once again men! Those of you who have made it back alive and those who unfortunately haven't, have proven once again that you are dedicated to defending your king and country, and although some of our brothers have fallen, I believe and continue to believe that with the work you all have put in, we will win this war. I would like to give a special recognition to Private Nowak, who has come so far from his first battle and continues to strive, well done Private." We were all dismissed, and Oliver and John congratulated me, "beating Peter at cards, recognition from the General, what's next?" John asked in high spirits, "knighthood," Oliver jested, we laughed as we made our way to tea.

It was a month before I received a letter from Claudia, but I didn't blame her as letters in the trenches were scarce from everyone. But when news did finally arrive from home it was not as pleasant as I had hoped.

Dear Sam,

I hate that this must be the first letter I write, but things have been rather hectic here since you both left. Bart misses you dearly and is asking when you will be back. For the first week he didn't sleep and at first, I thought he might have been having nightmares about the bombing but after I asked him, he said he wanted to wait for you coming home from work. I've tried explaining this all to him, but he is much too young. Once he saw Margaret again, he did go back to normal, thankfully.

Alex offered her again to come and stay with us, but she doesn't want to leave Branden alone, and honestly, I think he was relieved she said no, it seems he would be a bit lonely without them. However now that I remember the purpose of this letter, I think it's best I write it down now before I forget again. Last night Alex had severe pains in her stomach, so I took her to the hospital, and we got the unfortunate news that Alex had lost her baby.

She's fine as one can be in these circumstances, however she was told to stay in bed for the next few days, so Mary and I are taking turns in looking after both children so someone can look after Alex.

I'm sorry this must be the first letter I write to you but as you can imagine none of us have had a chance to write sooner. We all eagerly await your response.

With love, Claudia.

I kept this letter although it brought bad news as I feared it would have been the last, but as time went on it became a sentiment. To hear my sister lost her child drowned my own joy that I somehow found in this nightmare and my immediate reaction was to go to Oliver and break the news to him. "Mary told me in her letter. It's a shame, I hope she's doing as the doctor says,"
"me too, but I know Alex, she doesn't like to be looked after, I better write back. Do you know when they send the letters out,"
"Sundays. Let Alex know I'm thinking about her,"
"Will do," I replied and went to write my response.

To all the family,

It grieves me terribly to hear about this dreadful news. No one deserve such a tragedy, let alone Alex. But she is strong, and I know she will make it through the unimaginable pain she must be feeling.

After hearing this I have one favour to ask of both you, my sweetheart and Mary. I need you to do everything in you can to make sure my sister takes as much time as she needs to recover from this loss. I know my sister better than I know myself, even if you have to use force please keep her from pushing herself to work through this time without a sufficient time to recover.

Please keep writing and letting Oliver and I know of your own wellbeing. Coming home is our main motivation.

With love, Sam.

Once again, I had to wait a while to hear back from Claudia, but the anxiety I had towards my sister's wellbeing did not affect my performance on the battlefield. In the next week I was informed of Alex's recovery through that long-awaited letter.

Dear Sam,

You were right about Alex; she does try her hardest to do everything herself even though she knows she isn't well enough. Nevertheless, we managed to keep her in bed resting until recently when she was determined she was fit enough to move her rest to the sitting-room. We all saw an immediate change in her with this change of scenery and we felt more comfortable with her wandering about the garden which once again brought on a huge improvement.

However in other matters there was an incident with Branden, although I'm not too sure if Mary plans to tell Oliver in her letter so maybe keep this to yourself for a bit. As you know, the suffragettes have been doing a great job working towards woman's rights, Mary and I are even considering joining if we could find the time, however there is a group of woman from this movement who are giving them a bad name.

Mary and Branden were walking to the shop with the children, while I stayed at the estate with Alex. On their way they saw a man giving a couple of women a lot of verbal abuse, calling them all sorts and for the most part it seems unjustified however they weren't innocent in it all. Well you know what Branden is like when he sees someone in need his instinct is to help them, so he did. He called over to the young man, who according to Mary looked to be only fourteen or fifteen, and he told him he had no right talking to two young ladies that way and he should be off before he and his family came out of the shop.

The poor boy lost himself and when they were out, he was gone. However those women weren't and came straight up to him and gave him all sorts of nonsense about how he was a coward for not signing up and a real man would be fighting for his country. And then they stuck a white feather in the top buttonhole of his jacket. Poor Branden. He would do anything to fight alongside his son, but it's not certain he would be allowed to with his arthritis and his age, well he's nearly eighty.

The worst thing of it all is that he would never disrespect a lady no matter what, so he stood there and took it until Mary jumped in telling them they had no right to be talking to him like that and he wouldn't be allowed to even if he tried because he's ill, that shut them right up. But he is so upset over it all. He is too good a man to be treated like that.

Alex has organized for him and Mary to come to dinner at the estate and she's hired a professional chef to come in and cook for us too, but he doesn't know. It's to be a surprise to cheer him up.

I hope you're well and safe, please write back soon.

With love, Claudia

My blood boiled when hearing what happened to Branden, he didn't deserve that, and I hope no one, whether they are a young boy or old frail man decides to give into the taunting and join the front lines, for this is hell. I was relieved to hear that Mary stood up for him although I wasn't surprised. Hearing from my family so infrequently was hard but it only acted as a motivator to give every battle everything I had in hopes it would end soon.

In 1915, the war had not ended like we were told it would be and at this point it didn't feel like it was ever going to end.

CHAPTER SEVENTEEN

One morning, at early hours, I woke up to coughing and wheezing, and then as I became more conscious, I heard people screaming. The smell was putrid and I struggled to breathe through the thick clouds that plagued our trench, I was harassed suddenly by another soldier who was forcing a gas mask over my head, I wasn't able to recognise him as he was wearing a mask himself. In my half-conscious state I thought he was causing me harm, so I refused until I realized the reality that instead of trying to kill me, he was trying to save me. We had a gas attack. It was a smart decision to get us during a time when a large portion of us would be asleep and unexpecting. I staggered from the cove I was sleeping in and took a clouded and dozed look around the trenches where I saw thousands of men clutching their eyes and their faces. Those who weren't injured were shooting up at the enemy who stood at the edge of the trench, spraying us down with a form of deadly gas like we were rats and they the exterminators. Other men ran to the field and this is where I went. I grabbed my rifle and threw myself into the action.

Arms and legs and bits of flesh fell around me as blood flew from the bodies of the victims. The smell of death, sweat, blood and vomit had filled the field, not that I got such an intense smell of it because of the gas mask but it was strong enough that some seeped through. I used my gun mostly, I was shooting aimlessly and if I heard a dying scream, I assumed I hit someone, who I hit I did not know, the gas mask clouded my vision and everything that I saw looked like mists or silhouettes. I was only a few feet away from the enemy trenches when I came across a man from the opposing side that had lost his leg but still hung on to his last moments for as long as he could. I laughed in his face when I saw him, he looked so pathetic and when I was close enough, he sounded worse. He pleaded to me, but I could not understand a word. When I stared at him considering whether or not I would shoot him or spare him he then he realised I was with the English and he spoke it plain to me. "Kill me" he wheezed through his dying voice, "please kill me" he began to cry, "You'll die soon anyway, what's the point in me wasting a bullet on you?" I spat, "Have mercy" he cried sorely, "Mercy! What do you know about mercy you monster?" he fiddled with his front pocket on his shirt, I knew he was too weak to pull out a weapon, so I didn't feel the need to hesitate and instead knelt next to him. He held out to me a picture, I snatched it from him and saw a woman smiling with a child in her arms, on the back was a message written in his language, I asked him to read it to me, "Please come home, Franz. Love Otley and Ida. It is my sister and my niece." tears came to his eyes and his voice faded. He looked at me so hopeful, but I could never give him peace. For a second, I sympathised with him, but just a second. I ripped the photo into shreds and released it to the wind. "You don't need to carry around a useless piece of paper to keep your family with you. Keep them in your heart." I said as I pulled my gun in front of me and aimed it at his head, "Do you pray for them?" he nodded stiffly. "Look over them in heaven if you believe there is one, they'll join you soon enough" I said and shot him dead. Then I carried on.

I returned to the trenches soon after and immediately searched for Oliver. Corpses filled the trench in a neat row. After they were identified and tagged, they were covered with a sheet, but those who hadn't been tagged yet exposed the horrors of the attack. Men who's eyes were once brown were now glassy blue. Some had lost their noses, and some had large blisters covering a large part of their faces. It was hard to identify most of them but when I asked a medic for the names of who had been identified so far, among those was Alton Scott. I didn't think about him and hadn't since we met him at our arrival, but he was a good friend and helped me and my family a lot when I met him. "Which – which one is he?" I asked, "he's the third one at the end of this row," "will you come and find me if Oliver McCarthy turns up?"

"Private McCarthy?" I nodded feeling slightly panicked about what he was going to say next, "he's among the injured, they're at the end of this row as well. They'll be sent back to England tonight,"

"Oh, thank goodness. Is he badly injured?"

"Not much. He was shot in the shoulder but he's conscious, he's determined he's coming back. He won't be allowed though, not after an injury like that."

"thank you," I replied without acknowledging what he said at the end. I slowly made my way up the row of corpses. I didn't count them, but there must have been close to a thousand, and those that were covered didn't make up half of the total. Then I got to Alton. I had no interest in knowing his injuries, but I wished I knew how he passed, just so I could put to rest the uneasiness I had wondering if it was a slow and painful death. He didn't deserve this end, so far away from his family. I knelt at his feet and said I was sorry and bade him one final goodbye. I then went to find Oliver.

I found a nurse who was going around the injured checking off their names, "excuse me, I'm looking for Oliver McCarthy?"
"McCarthy? I don't think we've had a McCarthy" my heart sunk, "Do you know when he was injured?"
"I don't but the medic I just past said he was here,"
"A lot of the men who were injured during the gas attack have been sent back to England already."
"The medic said he was shot," the medic looked back down at his list, "Oh, wait no he was just checked. He's over there with those other gentlemen who have only minor injuries, you see them?" he pointed to a group of men sitting on crates, having surprisingly lively conversation for some who have been injured. His arm was hung in a sling and his torso was wrapped in bandages, "Sam!" he rejoiced, "I heard they are sending you home?" I asked him, "Yes, silly isn't it, this will clear up in no time. Nonetheless I'll be back in a couple of weeks."
"You can't be serious? You want to come back here?"
"The war hasn't been won yet Sam. I still have a job to do."
"The medic says you won't be allowed, and what about Mary. She'll be terrified if you come back,"
"She doesn't have a say in this Sam, I am fighting for my daughter's future."
"But Oliver you're injured! And this is hell"
"Does it matter? This is my country and my family's country and yours to. What right do I have to? succumb to my injuries like a coward?"
"You'll not be a coward if you allow yourself a rest. Mary will need you at home."
"But my country needs me here."
"You're not a coward, you're just an idiot," I said and stormed off.

I knew I could count on Mary to keep him home. When he was taken back to England he was immediately hospitalized, and his injuries were treated. However he was constantly talking about his return, so the doctors, out of concern for his mind and life more than the recovery of his injury, prolonged his stay in the hospital as long as possible. Although I thought Lewes hospital was cursed, I had faith that Mary, Claudia and Alex would make sure nothing would happen to him. My next letter from Claudia and every letter since was an update on Oliver. And each one kept me going, now that I didn't have my brother to motivate me.

My dear Sam,

Oliver is slowly making progress in his recovery. They originally sent him to a hospital in London, but we moved him out of the city and closer to us. Alex says he's in the hospital your mother worked for. He is much happier in here as well since he is surrounded by familiar faces. Mary still won't give into the idea of him re-joining when he is fully recovered and I can't lie I am glad she won't, I would hate it if you came home as Oliver has. Margaret hasn't been able to visit him yet as Mary doesn't want her seeing him while he's in such horrible pain.

Alex almost seems fully recovered from her own loss, she tells me that her and Andrew will try again when he returns and although her first will always be in her heart she knows the child is in heaven now and living a much better life with your mother. We still haven't heard anything of Andrew, which I must confess, it concerns me for Alex's sake but he is at sea so I believe that may be why. But at the same time, it's been two years and the only letter she received was one that he sent while still in training. She wants me to tell you in this letter that you are making her so proud, and I must say it is shared among all of us here.

As you know Bart has started school and I'm not too sure when you'll receive this letter but yesterday, from the day that I write this was his first day. You should have seen him; he would have made you so proud. The day before was a nightmare as he didn't want to go without you, but I told him that you were away fighting for the country and that you were a hero. So when he went into his first day, he told his teacher, "my dad's a hero". You make us all proud.

Poor Margaret though, she was a bit shyer and more wanted to play with Bart and Bart alone, but he had a new group of friends and said that they didn't want to play with girls. I told him to include her more, but we'll see what happens tomorrow.

Anyway, I hope you are safe and well and I hope this will be over soon so you can return to us.

With love, Claudia.

I could have read her letters over and over for hours, her words brought such comfort to me. I wrote back immediately and eagerly awaited her response. However every time I wrote a letter now, I had Peter and John leaning over me asking me to let Oliver know they were thinking of him and to give their love to his and my family. A strange pair, but they made a decent substitute to Oliver's company.

Dear Claudia,

I can't express the amount of comfort your letters bring

me. I read them over and over every night and every day when I have some time to spare.

Please tell Mary that I completely and utterly agree with her that Oliver should not return, and if it means I have to put in the extra time to end this war myself I will. He is a stubborn fellow though just like his dad, how is Branden doing? I'm sure he's glad Oliver's home.

There's no news I can give you of life out here as nothing new has happened. The same old routine day after day. It makes me all the more eager to come home. I have John and Peter leaning over my shoulder asking for me to let Oliver know they're thinking of him and want to give their love to his family. They said they would love to grab a pint with him when they get home.

Make sure you tell Bart that I said he must include Margaret with his new friends, they're more or less siblings they should act like that.

I hope you know that I love you and think about returning to my family every day,

With love, Sam

Oliver never fully recovered from his injuries, but in 1917 he was convinced he had and tried to sign up again, he was rejected of course. And the next letter I received from Claudia was all the details of his tantrum afterwards. I've never been able to understand his eagerness for the battle, but I don't think he enjoyed war as much as making his family proud. I remained close to Peter and John but soon they would disappear just like the other men before them. It seemed like time went on everything got harder, like it was a game of musical chairs, but the losers were either dead or injured. Peter was the first to go. There was another gas attack, but he didn't manage to get his mask on in time, so the gas had filled his lungs and suffocated him. Then it was John, but he didn't die, he was only injured. Only is an under-statement, he lost his leg. I will spare you the details. Once they were gone it's fair to say I had given up, but I still gave every battle my all.

I charged on to the battlefield with the men I learned to see as my brothers. Our enemies were becoming smaller and smaller with every battle but so were we. I shot wildly not paying attention as to where I was shooting but I knew that I had at least hit someone. Again, I was surrounded by flying limbs and guts and the screams of dying and fighting men was all I could hear over the explosions of gunfire and grenades. The smell of death swam around me making me nauseous once again. But before I could understand my surroundings I was suddenly struck by a bullet in my knee. I always wondered how painful a gun shot was. I saw how it could kill men and bring them down at once, but I never imagined it feeling like this. It was excruciating. The adrenaline kept me awake through it all as the pain burst through my body and touched every nerve. In one second, I was one of those men who were screaming. I felt the blood flow from the back of my knee and the front. I felt every drip as it slipped down my leg, there was so much of it. I couldn't look, because I thought if I looked the pain or the blood loss would kill me. I could feel myself screaming but I couldn't hear it. All I heard was my pulse beating hard and fast. I knew I was dying. When I lost hope of being saved, I prayed, "Please, dear lord, forgive me!" I cried out "I should never have lost faith I know that now! Please have mercy!" as I said this last line I was welcomed by a bright light before everything went black. Was this hell? Did God have no mercy? Was I being punished for each sin I committed?

CHAPTER EIGHTEEN

I woke up, to my despair, in the hospital of death. Although Oliver lived, I had no faith in myself being able to defeat its curse. I was surrounded by my closest friends and my family. All of them sleeping around my bed. I had no idea of the time or day, and I had no clue what happened. All I did know was my knee was in terrible agony. A nurse came in, and to my delightful shock I recognised t her from somewhere deep in my past. I hope my reader will recall Claire; she was the wonderful woman who took care of us in our young years after the death of my mother. I had no idea when I left for university that to find her, I would have to look in the one place I feared the most for her. "Oh, your awake, that's good, your friends have been waiting for you to wake up a while." she whispered, her voice still sounded angelic and delightfully peaceful. "This lot hasn't left your side since you got here, you're very lucky,"

"I am indeed. But Claire, don't you recognise me?" she looked at the name on my chart then looked back up at me in dumbstruck, "oh, my goodness, Sam!" she said just loud enough to wake up everyone else in the room, I shook Alex gently to get her attention quickly, "Alex, look, it's Claire!" she looked at the nurse in shock, "Oh my! I can't believe I didn't recognise you!" she stood up to embrace our old nanny, "Me neither, but you both are so grown up now, I only knew you when you were children,"

"What she's trying to say Sam is your old" Oliver joked, everyone chuckled, "I don't know what that says about you, your birthday is before mine" I replied, "Oh Sam I'm so pleased you're awake." said Claudia "As am I. Claire please may I introduce my wife Claudia, my best friend Oliver and his wife Mary, and Bart my son who is asleep over there in the bed," Claire began to tear up, "I can't believe you are married and have a child, I've missed so much."

"It isn't entirely your fault I did move to London."

"London! Oh, my goodness no wonder you came here! It's not safe all the way in London I've been told the town is in ruins."

"When the first bombs went off we hid in the train station, thankfully the some people thought ahead and turned it into an air raid shelter, the morning after we all came to Lewes, Alex has been so kind as to host Bart and I in her and Andrew's estate." Claudia added.

"Well I'm so glad you did or else I don't think our paths would ever cross again. But Sam, what are you doing joining the army?" I looked at Oliver and raised an eyebrow, after all it was his idea. "I knew you were going to get him into trouble at some point," Claire stated to Oliver and we all broke out into laughter. "Well anyway Sam how are you feeling? Is your leg giving you any pain?"

"Just a little, but I'm alright. What has happened? Is the war over?" they all looked down in shame and guilt, "Unfortunately not Sam, you were shot, and they sent you home." Claudia was the one to break the news,

"Not so fun is it? Not being able to go back and finish what you started" Oliver joked but I was in no mood for jokes. "I'll let the doctor know your leg is causing you pain and he'll be in to check it. I should probably give you all some privacy right now."
"Please Claire don't be a stranger" said Alex, "I won't, don't worry Alex" she replied and left the room.

Once she was gone, I felt more comfortable with putting Oliver back in his place, "we didn't start this; we were forced into it." I snapped at Oliver who was of course persistent in joining back. "Nonetheless we got ourselves involved and now we have to finish it. We need to end the war because we're men, and that's what men are supposed to do."
"Oliver, I love you like a brother, so believe me when I say that I mean this with kindness, but you are a fool."
"You two shouldn't be fighting right now, you need to rest Sam, and Oliver you shouldn't be provoking him" Claudia included, Mary nodded in agreement. We dropped the subject for the time being, but it was not the last time he tried to sway me. Alex then shared some tragic news with us, "I got a telegram yesterday, the one that was brought here" she said, and Claudia nodded at her with a look of concern, "It was from the navy. Andrew was killed in action. They couldn't identify him straight away because he didn't have his identification tags. But it was soon after he left his training." she could say no more but what she said sounded so cold, like she could not allow herself to feel the full extent of the words she spoke. Claudia broke down with her and went over to comfort her. "Alex, I'm so, so sorry. I cannot imagine the pain you must be feeling right now."
"I'm just pleased that you have returned to us safe, although harmed. I could not bear to lose my brother alongside my husband and child."

"I promise that everyday my health permits I will fight to stay in this world with you. I hope you can believe me regardless of the past" a bold statement that was now that I think of it. Nevertheless she nodded and I held her hand. The children woke up and Bart, after seeing I was awake, jumped of the bed to mine and hugged me tightly, something I thought I would never get to experience again, "now Bart, be careful, your dad has a sore leg."
"No, Claudia it's fine, let him stay."

Oliver and Mary left soon after the children woke up as they Margaret was getting bored and began acting out, "I'm really sorry Sam but we're going to have to get Margaret home," said Oliver who picked his daughter up with his good arm and grabbed her coat with the other, "Don't be sorry, I understand,"
"We can take Bart if you like?" offered Mary, Claudia looked to me for a response, "it's alright, let him stay" I said not willing to give up a second of my son's presence. The doctor came in a good couple of hours after them, understandable due to the number of patients he must have had with more important health concerns than mine. He cleared the room. He did a few check-ups and asked me if it hurt when I moved it this way and that, when I confirmed he looked gravely concerned. "I am so sorry Mr Nowak, but I don't think you will be able to regain full function of your knee and may have to use a cane from now on." he said with a dead tone, like he was handing out a jail sentence to a convict and that was what annoyed me the most about his attitude, because I wasn't a convict I was a soldier, I had just fought in a war and now the quality of my life has been limited and he talks about it like it's nothing. "You say that so emotionless, is that not a bad thing?" I said with the most attitude I could build up in my voice without having melted. "I am sorry Mr Nowak but

when you have treated as many soldiers as I have, and you have had to break the news that they wouldn't make it past the week or their leg would need to be amputated or they will never see or hear properly again, you lose your sense of empathy." he said and then left the room allowing my family to return. I summarised the check up with them, "he said I will lose some of my function in my knee and will have to use a crutch." "That doesn't mean that you won't walk again," Claudia said with an air of positivity which I couldn't seem to share. I sat silent.

Once I was released from the hospital, I was prescribed pain killers and weekly physiotherapy. The doctors worked hard with me to get my knee back to full function, but after a month of physical therapy the best I could do with was a limp. Claudia quietly hated the cane for a time because it aged me way beyond my thirty-six years, but she would never say anything to me, she was too afraid to hurt me. While Oliver and I worked out a plan in terms of employment my family stayed with Alex and his with Branden. With the paper being destroyed and London still being unsafe to live in, I struggled with what to do next. Alex never rushed me to move out of the estate, I think she was afraid to live on her own. As time went on, I saw her demeanour change from content to depressed. She used to always wear a smile but now it was rare to ever see one reach her face. And then it happened. On the 11th of November 1918 Germany had surrendered and the war had ended. When the news was broadcasted we all sat silently doing our own thing in Alex's sitting-room, Claudia read, Bart and Margaret played together on the floor, Mary was making a quilt for Alex who was also reading, Branden had fallen asleep and Oliver and I, as per usual, sat contentedly listening to the radio. When the news broke that the allies won the war after

Germany's surrender, we all gasped in unison. Such news came as a well needed relief to all who suffered its consequences. But as much as we were relieved, we couldn't entirely believe it. "Is it true?" Mary blurted, "it must be, why else would they put it over the radio. Dad? dad! Wake up, wake up."

"What's the matter? Is Lewes being attacked now?"

"No dad not at all, we've won the war! Typical it all happens as soon as we leave," Oliver joked, and it was the most wonderful joke I had ever heard. "After all this time we have finally won, can you believe it Mary?" Claudia embraced Mary. Margaret wanted to be involved in the excitement, so she pulled on her mother's dress for her attention, Mary picked her up and Oliver went over to kiss them both. Bart wasn't as curious as Margaret but did want his mother to pick him up also to feel included. Alex, although relieved, didn't share in our joy, seeing that I tried to comfort her, "think of it this way Alex, his death was not a waste. He fought for his country and his country has won, he will be one among the many who will be put down in history as a hero." I said sitting beside her on the couch, "You're right Sam, but it's hard."

"I know," I put my arm around her and sat while the others celebrated, I was over-joyed, but I didn't want her to suffer, or to be alone. Out of nowhere there was cheering in the streets only minutes after the news had broken. "Sam you should see this, it looks like the whole towns out celebrating. Why don't we go join them?" Oliver had said while getting his family's coats. "I'll meet you out there I'm going to sit with Alex for a bit."

"Are you sure Sam?" asked Claudia, "Of course, but you go with Mary and Oliver, Claudia, it is the end of the war after all," they ran outside to join the town, Bart and Margaret included.

Alex leaned her head on my shoulder and we were alone in the silence and gloom of the sitting-room while the rest of England celebrated, "Sam, when I look around this house that my husband obtained and provided for our family, I see strangers. I don't know Claudia or Oliver and I certainly do not know Oliver's wife or dad. The only relations I have in this home is you and my nephew, but you both are more a part of the rest of your family than you are with me"

"That's nonsense Alex, Claudia sees you as a sister, not just her sister-in-law but her sister. And you're my blood, we grew up together, we share the same tragedies. You and I are as close as any two people can be/"

"Regardless this is my dead husbands' home where we were supposed to raise our dead child and now it is filled with strangers, even you feel like a stranger to me sometimes."

"Alex don't say things like that. We're family. Why don't you come out and celebrate the end of the war with the rest of them, that will cheer you up."

"I want to take Hanna out of the hospital, it's been four years and I haven't had so much as a letter updating me on her well-being. Surely she's better now." I didn't exactly agree with Alex's decision to take Hanna home, but I could not say no to her anymore. "If you want to take Hanna out of the hospital, I will be more than happy to help you in any way I can. You're right, she should be better now, and we should make an inquiry as to why we've had no word of her health. But in the meantime, why don't you come out to the celebration?" she nodded, and we went out together into the crowd of the cheerful people of England but neither of us were as cheery.

CHAPTER NINETEEN

After the celebrations, people immediately began rebuilding everything they lost. Training centres were opened up for those who fought to help us get back to our lives. But nothing was the same. Oliver refused to speak of his time in the trenches, not even with me. If anyone asked, he would say it was a nightmare and would change the subject to something completely different. According to Mary he wasn't sleeping and struggled doing things he would usually find no problem with. One day she came to Alex's estate where we were staying with Margaret, in tears, "Sam, please you have to speak to Oliver, he's lost his mind," she pleaded as she entered the sitting-room, I stood up and bid her take my seat next to Claudia, "what's happened?" I asked "Margaret was playing with her dolls in the kitchen while I was making lunch. I asked her to get me a plate to start serving, I forgot Branden's dishes were in the top cupboard, so she stood on a chair, I had my back turned so I didn't see her. The chair slipped and Margaret fell, she only had a bump on her knees, but Oliver shot through to the kitchen from the sitting-room. He looked at me, but it was like he wasn't seeing me, and he shot across the room and started choking me. Margaret screamed and Branden came through and pulled him off me. He was so sorry, but I was so scared. So I left."

"You were right to do so Mary, Margaret, why don't you go play with Bart in the garden?" Claudia responded and looked at me, "I'll go speak to him, but please understand Mary, there's not many men who came back from that hell unscathed. If we don't have physical scars, we have other scars that can't be treated. Please forgive him," she nodded, and I left for Branden's.

"Sam! Oliver's not feeling too well," Branden said flatly, "I know, Mary came to see us. Can I speak to him," he opened the door to let me in, "he's upstairs, in his room, he won't talk to me," I made my way up the staircase and knocked on the door, there was no answer. I walked straight in to see Oliver with his head in his hands sitting on the bed, "Oliver?" I said quietly, he didn't move or respond, "how are you?" I asked, not sure how else to proceed, he began to sob. "Mary isn't angry with you; I think she understands."

"She can't understand"

"She's trying, that's the main thing, do you want to tell me what happened,"

"Why? Mary's obviously told you already,"

"But that doesn't explain what went on in your mind," he looked at me with the same empty stare I saw in most soldiers, it's like they're looking right through you rather than at you, I wonder if I had the same. "I don't know what happened. I only remember my dad pulling me off her. The memory of that is mixed with a memory from the field." I sat next to him on the bed and put my arm over him in comfort. He sobbed harder, "I'm sorry Oliver, you don't deserve to be suffering like this, but maybe when things get back to normal, you'll feel better," he didn't respond but I didn't press him.

I was right about Oliver, he got a position in the first firm he worked at, since many of the other employees were killed during the war there was a lot of vacancies to fill, and I believe it was the familiarity of the routine that helped him feel better. We all decided to stay in Lewes as London was in ruins for a long time after the war and there was no indication when it would be safe to move back. Once Oliver got his job secured, he moved into a larger house, one close to the size of his old one in London but it had an extra room because both him and Mary wanted another child. During one of our visits to Oliver's new home he offered me a position in his firm. We were in his study when he asked, "have you considered what you'll do now?"
"I don't know, not many of the newspapers are taking on new workers. Maybe it's time I use this degree I have,"
"You sure?" he asked slightly amused, "no, but I need to move out of Alex's house at some point."
"Well if you want you can come and work at my firm?"
"Really? Are you sure?"
"Absolutely! Can you start Monday?" I won't lie I was not looking forward to starting a job in law, and Oliver after the first week of my new job. Nonetheless I was able to afford a new house in Lewes, one just as big as Oliver's and we moved in that same day. But I think he saw my lack of interest slowly making its way to the surface, as I struggled to keep the strong momentum I had when I was an editor. When we were sitting in my study, I realise now he was trying to convince me to reconsider it, "I don't understand Sam, you were so dead against it after you became an editor, and no offence but you're not very good at it either."

"I know, but I have the degree, and these are different times, I must find a way to provide for my family more than I did as an editor, and law is the only way I can do that."
"Why don't you write a book?"
"Ha! A book? About what?"
"Your experience during the war, show people what it was actually like for us, in the front lines"
"I'll start writing books again when you start writing poetry again."
"Okay, you made your point there, but are you sure you want to be a lawyer?"
"Of course I do, I would do anything for my family and being a lawyer is the best thing for them."
"Very well, but that actually reminds me of something I wanted to talk to you about. My dad keeps going on about how he is giving us the house when he's gone. It's a morbid conversation and I don't want to think of him not being with me. Do people talk about the end when they're about to die?"
"I am not too sure Oliver; my mother's death was sudden and my fathers... it was expected but we weren't close, and he never spoke a word when we went to visit him in the hospital. But your mum did, and your dad's old. His wife is gone, his children are getting older, it's not surprising he is thinking of the end." "Ach, you're probably right, I'm just" he sighed "I don't think I could handle that kind of grief again just yet."
"I promise you Oliver that it will be hard in the beginning, but it will slowly get easier. You will still have your family to take care of, they'll get you through once again. But you never know, maybe Branden will out-live all of us" we smiled at each other.

Alex waited until Bart was out of the house before she went to get Hanna, but when the time came wasn't able to take Hanna home. I went with her to the hospital to sign any papers I needed to sign and to drive them home. But when we got to the hospital, we were told Hanna's condition only worsened during the war and she was put away to a secure unit. The nurse we spoke to looked completely uninterested when we inquired after our sister, "What's the last name?" she sighed as she flicked through the folder with the names of the patients, "Nowak" Alex said, trying to be as polite as possible in spite of the nurses rudeness, "I don't see her name," the nurse concluded, Alex looked at me, panicked, "she has to be here, we brought her here before the war," she rolled her eyes, "do you know the date? Or the year at least?"

"It was 1914," Alex responded hopeful, "I'll have to go speak to the doctor, please wait here," she left the desk and went into an office where the doctor was. She returned soon after with him, "Mr Nowak," he began, "I must apologise. Your sister, Hanna had to be transferred to a secure unit soon after she was committed, you should have received a letter but there's a chance it was delayed due to the circumstances,"

"Can't we take her home?" I inquired both eager and enraged, "I'm afraid not, your sister is… well the lights are on but no one's home. To take her out of our care would be dangerous for both the public and herself. You are welcome to come and see her?" I was about to take this offer to see Hanna, but Alex broke when she heard the news. She collapsed in a pool of tears on the hospital floor and I had to pick her up and take her out of the building, as the hospital employees were having none of it. When I took her home, she immediately went to her bedroom, and slept. I stayed with her until she woke again and told me to leave. Now all the company she has is her maid and a cook, but she permits no one else to see her. The people of Lewes now call her that lady in the estate, as if she didn't have a name. It hurts me so much to see people dehumanize my sister Alex.

I knew I wouldn't like life as a lawyer, but if I knew I would hate it as much as I did, I would not have allowed myself to get trapped into such an awful career. I think Claudia was the first to notice my change of character. How ignorant I was to her feelings, how easy it was to push myself over the edge causing, to my shame, violent outbursts just like my own dad. As Bart got older, I was less and less involved in his life due to the demanding schedule of the firm. This was the worst part of it, not being able to watch my only child grow up, but even when I was there, I wasn't fully. Once Bart had turned nine and began spending more time with his friends than her, I saw she began to feel lonely, but I had no time to fill in for him. One day as I was drowning in the paperwork I brought home in my study she came to me, seeking a solution for her loneliness, "Sam, I would like to talk to you for a moment." she said as if she was tiptoeing around me, "what?" I snapped, she took the seat beside the bookshelf, I used as a reading nook, or rather another way to isolate myself from my family, it was also the farthest from my desk, "Bart is getting so big now don't you think?" I stayed silent, not giving her the courtesy of so much as a glance, "did you know Mary and Oliver were trying?" I don't know why I didn't see what came next, perhaps I was too busy to pay attention to my wife, "do you think we could have another child?" she asked apprehensively, and rightly so, there was no telling how I would have reacted at this time and how I did react only proved the worse, "Why on earth would you want that at a time like this?" I spat, "You have been very stressed recently, and maybe a baby would motivate you to take some time for yourself... and your family. You were so happy when Bart was born and-"

"Bart was born in a different time,"
"But you could make more time for a new baby, I'm sure Oliver would be more than happy to give you the time off." I don't know what had happened but when she said Oliver, I saw red. I had sprung from my chair at my desk and bolted across the room. I grabbed her arms, screaming in her face, "if you think Oliver has that much power over me, you are wrong! Don't you ever say something as stupid as that again!" she quivered in my hands, tears streaming from her eyes. I threw her back on the chair and walked out of the study, Bart was standing at the door staring at me with wide eyes, he was still only a child but I may have ruined that for him "get back to your room now!" I bellowed at him then I walked out the house and went to the pub, just like my father did.

I was so ashamed of myself, but that shame was outweighed by the embarrassment that prevented me, until drunk enough, to crawl back to Claudia and beg her to forgive me. It didn't take me long to down as many whiskey's as I could, and the world became blurry, so I stumbled home. I knocked as I wasn't sure if she had locked the door and I was too intoxicated to think to check, and in a way, I wanted to give her back some power against me and my new demon. When she opened the door, I could see how angry she was, and I knew how badly I ruined my relationship with her. Unlike my mother she wasn't easily persuaded to forgive once she had been wronged. Looking upon her face and seeing the woman I loved that angry because of my own terrible action, made me cry. Why did I cry?
"I'm so sorry Claudia" I slurred, "Please forgive me"
"Why?"
"Because I'm your husband, and I'm Bart's father, I'm so sorry Claudia. I haven't been myself recently."
"I know that, Samuel, and I have been trying to tell you

that for a while now."

"I know, and I haven't been listening when I should have been. But I promise, I will listen now. I will take some time off from work, and if you want a baby, we will have a baby. Please let me make it better." I pleaded but she looked at me with the most heart-wrenching look of disappointment, but she let me in. I was too drunk to make it upstairs with her, not that I think Claudia would have let me upstairs with her, so I fell asleep on the couch with the intention to make it up to her as soon as possible. The next morning, I woke up an hour before I was supposed to leave for work, and I made both her and Bart a large feast for a breakfast. I let her sleep in so I could write an apology note and I wouldn't have to see her angry face and went off to work. I didn't confess to Oliver about my outburst to Claudia or how the work could be affecting me in a negative way, and although I did say to Claudia, I would talk to Oliver about giving me time off, instead I piled through the work that I was tasked with and took on more. Although we were both working for this firm, we saw each other less and less as time went on. Our families were close, but it didn't feel like we were anymore. A lot had to be done after the war to rebuild England after so much destruction had been done, and I don't think anyone expected lawyers to be so involved in that. But Oliver had a lot more work to do representing companies in court and having meetings so frequently, since I wasn't as good at that I was tasked with rebuilding the firm alongside the other employees. My apology note had won with Claudia and she kept me on the condition that I never acted out again, "Claudia, I am undeserving of you truly," I rejoiced and kissed

"I know. I'm going to see Mary later this week, I would like to invite them up for dinner on Sunday." she stated, "I think that would be wonderful, we need some

normality in our lives once again" I lied, but it made Claudia smile and it was a smile full of hope for our future, hope that I shared for a time, just through seeing her so pleased with me. She didn't ask me about work or if I told Oliver that I needed time off, so I didn't tell her, that way I thought at least I wasn't lying to her. In a way I think she already knew that I didn't tell him and each day I went back she still refrained from asking.
I counted down the days to Sunday and invited Oliver personally while I was at work with him, he too, was excited to get back to our old routine. I think he felt what I felt but there was a lot more pressure on him since he was so high up in the firm. That Sunday started off well, I helped Claudia make some of the dinner and Bart played quietly with us in the kitchen with the new set of toy soldiers I bought him on my way home from work the day before. The best thing about Sundays at this period in history was that no one worked, so I had the whole day to spend with my family. After we prepared some of dinner we sat in the sitting-room, I played with Bart and his toys while Claudia read, and the radio was on in the background. My family were mine once again. It was a perfect day until I ruined it.

CHAPTER TWENTY

Immediately when it hit noon I began to down glasses of whisky against Claudia's wishes, the more I drank the more confident I felt and I didn't think so much about the time I wasted fighting wars that wasn't mine and working a job that I didn't want. It also meant I could face Oliver who appeared to me my competition for the position of the man in my family. When Oliver and Mary came in, I can safely say I completely destroyed my marriage. Oliver and I, as per usual went into the study where he told me Branden had passed away on Friday, "Oliver, you really need to stop bringing bad news to Sunday dinners" I joked insensitively, "Well Sam you don't really give me any other opportunity,"
"Tell me something Oliver do you believe in heaven?"
"Of course, I do," I looked up to the ceiling and shouted, "You were right Branden, it meant war." Oliver laughed uncomfortably thinking I was just joking but he knew deep down there was something wrong. "How are you and Claudia?" he asked going

straight to the root of the problem which angered me for reasons that I knew deep inside weren't true but I was too drunk to accept, "She wants another child" I answered flatly "And you don't?"
"Now isn't the time to be bringing children into this world, especially with the little time I have already."
"I would give you the time off, Sam." he said too quickly, "if you did decide to have another child with Claudia." the same rage that burned within me when Claudia said it returned, but this time I could hold in my anger, "thank you, Oliver, but I'm not ready to raise another child. There is still so much we need to do in terms of getting back to normal" I could see he knew I was just making excuses, "well as long as you know the offer is always there, baby or not. You do a lot for your family already; it hasn't been easy for anyone returning from the front lines. It changes you Sam. You can't tell if you're a man or a monster or nothing at all." what he said made sense, but I didn't want to let myself accept how much sense it made.

When we sat down to dinner, I for some reason made it my mission to make everyone as uncomfortable as I was. I ate like an animal, mouth wide open as I chewed loudly, Bart thought it was funny, but I wasn't doing it for him. Margaret averted her eyes and asked her mum what I was doing, Mary told her I wasn't feeling well. I was drunk of course; I couldn't tell you a day I wasn't at this point. "So, Claudia, Oliver said he would give me the time off to have another child." she looked at me with extreme caution. "You are planning to have another baby? Claudia that is wonderful!" Mary exclaimed, "We spoke about it, but we aren't sure." Bart sat silently at his plate across from Margaret, although they were only children, they knew something was wrong, I saw it in their young faces. I think everyone knew, in a way I hoped everyone knew. I was

struggling and no one seemed to understand what.
"Aren't I so lucky Mary? My wife wants to give me a child and my best friend has given me permission to have one."
"Sam, is there something wrong?"
"Nothing wrong Oliver, nothing at all, except my wife sees you as more of a man than her own husband. Isn't that right Claudia?"
"Sam, I think it's best we drop the subject."
"Oh, look at him. Giving me orders. Sir, yes sir!" I said saluting him as if he were the General, "Claudia, you have made a beautiful meal, but I don't think our presence here is appropriate right now." Oliver stood up but I didn't let him be the bigger man. "No, what you mean to say is my presence is not appropriate right now, so sit back down, enjoy the meal my wife has made for you, I will leave." I stormed out of the house and off to the pub again.

When I came home I found Oliver and Mary stayed with Claudia, it must have been one o'clock in the morning when I managed to pull my nearly paralysed body to the front door, Instead of being polite I grunted and made my way to my study, the only good thing that came out of being a lawyer was having a big enough house that allowed plenty of space to escape to. Oliver followed me, "Sam you really need to figure out what is wrong with yourself and fix it because that was shameful." "Oh, don't start"
"Don't start? Sam, look at yourself, you're ruined, you have everything and you're wasting it all." he threw on my desk a journal, the same journal that I write in today, "you are not meant to be a lawyer; you need to recognise that"
"Writing is not a man's career, it is for pansies, and so is hiding from your problems in a fairy-tale." Oliver scoffed at my remark, "I have never heard your dad's

voice more clearly than I have just there. You were a man until now. Your son is afraid of you and your wife is ashamed. Is that what a man is Samuel? Someone too afraid to fix themselves so they've terrorized their family! Get yourself together Samuel." he left with Mary and Margaret and went home, leaving the house silent and dead. Claudia had told me she wanted me out of the house as soon as I packed my things the next again morning, I don't know how I convinced her to give me one more chance but by some miracle I did. Not that it would have mattered eventually whether I lived there or on the street.

As time went on, I didn't allow myself a moments rest after Oliver's offer just to spite him. Instead, I took on extra hours with the excuse that I needed the money so one day we would be ready for the child Claudia wanted. But I was already dead certain that I didn't want another child and at this point she wouldn't let me anywhere near her anyway. I didn't come home most nights; I spent the whole time at the pub. I made good friends with the workers and the other men who were regulars there, I was closer to them than my family. The day Oliver noticed my drinking had gotten bad was the day he couldn't keep me on at his firm. I don't blame him at all, even though we were almost like brothers, I couldn't allow him to lose his job because of me. "Sam, look, I don't want to have to do this, but you look terrible. When is the last time you went home?" "I don't remember" I slurred, "Well at least your honest. I am so sorry Sam, but I did tell you law wasn't for you. I'm going to have to let you go."
"I'm not surprised. You persevered long enough. Thank you, Oliver." I packed my things and left but this time I went straight home. All those extra hours I worked came into good use, because at least I had enough money to sustain a comfortable living while I searched

for other work. You may wonder why I didn't resent Oliver after this. It's because although I lived in an intoxicated haze, I knew he was not to blame.

When I went home to tell Claudia I had been let go, it only increased the resentment she had for me already for not coming home after work for the days prior. It must have been close to two weeks since I saw her before this then, "Sam, I can't believe you've done this to us!" she was sobbing hard, "I am so sorry" I slurred "what good is sorry now!" she cried. "You have to do something. Maybe if you clean up and sober up and talk to Oliver, he will take you back. Sam? Samuel!" I must have fallen asleep because I only remember hearing her shout my name and nothing else before it. She made me leave, which she had every right to do. I was useless now, just a drunken fool that wasted every opportunity he got that he didn't deserve. I went to Oliver's in seek for a place to stay before I could get back to my old self once again, I don't know why I thought he would have accepted me after everything I did. He was working for the rest of the day so I waited at the pub and told everyone how my wife just left me, I must have seemed so pathetic to them. At the end of Oliver's shift I had one more glass and went to his house, preparing a speech to convince him to let me stay. However when I got there, "she's left me" was all I could say and I hardly said more than slurred it, making it sound like one word. He let me in.

Mary wasn't pleased. I could hear them arguing about me in the next room after he helped me through to the couch in the sitting-room. "He is not staying here with Margaret. Claudia would never just throw him out if he did not become completely unbearable"
"Mary, I have to let him stay, I'm the reason he just lost his job."

"You did nothing, he did that all on his own"
"Please Mary, give the man a chance, he's like a brother to me, and he just needs to find his footing again. That war changed all of us, he's not himself right now. He just needs some help," there was a long silence, "Oliver McCarthy you are too kind." So, Oliver had his way and I was Oliver and Mary's guest for a time while I tried to get back to my old self. I didn't take anything from my house so the next again morning, Mary went to pick up some clothes and I later learned Oliver asked her to pick up the journal he gave me that I left on my desk. I'm sure while she was there Claudia told her everything and they both had a good gossip about me. I left a large sum for Claudia and Bart to live off while I was gone, and I kept the faith that one day I would be back with a better job than I had as a lawyer.

During my time as Oliver and Mary's guest I wasn't allowed to do as much as look at a drink, not that either of them drank since Margaret was born. I respected this rule as I knew they were going above and beyond for me and were doing more than I deserved. I looked for jobs outside of law, but I was stubborn enough to not do as much as pick up a pencil and write in this journal before now. I went to the newspaper agency that was outside of Lewes, as a penniless veteran and I practically begged them to take me on. They must have pitied me because they gave me the job and said it was because of my past experience before the war. I was once again an editor working for a newspaper, this time, only thirty minutes outside of Lewes. "Isn't that great Mary?" asked Oliver after I told him about my new job, "It is wonderful, have you told Claudia yet?" Mary responded and sounded genuinely happy for me, "I want to wait until I get my first wage so I can come home with something to offer,"
"Smart man!" Oliver patted my back, "how will we

celebrate?" he asked looking between Mary and me. We decided to go out for dinner and Mary left Margaret with Claudia.

For the first few issues of the paper the main topic was the war and the political aftermath. It was despairing to see so many photos of the damage that still remained four years after the war had ended, it brought back so many horrible memories of those days I spent in the trenches, the sorrowful moans of those who had been injured that echoed from throughout the trench and kept you awake all night, the wretched smells of the blood mixed in with the damp dirt and the sweat of those poor soldiers facing nightmares of the inescapable battlefield. It wasn't the best time to be a veteran editor when every piece written by those who did not fight in the war, was about war. It was like being cursed to relive your nightmares over and over for the rest of your life. I wanted to run from it, but I stayed for Claudia and Bart. For the most part it was bearable but then they asked me to write my own story, to be published in the paper, about what it was truly like to fight in the war, I was unsure how to proceed. The head editor had come to my desk one morning, grinning like a fool. Alton was very rarely without a smile, but he was nothing like this idiot. I think he thought it made him more approachable but for me it was just scary, like he was waiting to stab you in the back as soon as you turned away, "you've done some great work since you started," he began, but his voice had no purpose and was filled with fake enthusiasm, whether he actually believed I did "great work" was a mystery, "thank you sir," I responded awkwardly, "please Sam, call me Ben. I was wondering if you would care to take on an extra project for the next issue. There will of course be a bonus in it for you," I agreed only because it felt better to always be at work and with the bonus I could win back Claudia, "I would be more than happy to," I responded, "great! I was wondering if you could write a short story about what it was really like to be in the trenches." I should have mentioned that Ben was only twenty and the reason he was so high up in the agency was because when his dad went off to fight, he took over for him. "I'm not too sure I could do that hell justice." I responded, not so much out of modesty but because of the way that this request tied my stomach in a knot, "nonsense," he replied, "I'll need it in by next Monday, okay?" he didn't wait for my response and instead walked away. So I decided I had no choice to write this short story, but I would write it the best way I could without returning to my old alcoholic self.

The next Monday I handed it in and as he read over it, I could see he wasn't impressed, the problem they had was, although I wrote about the war, I wrote about the war and made it more interesting and enjoyable. The war I wrote about was that of men fighting monsters then turning into monsters themselves, "Sam, this isn't what we wanted."

"That's what it was like to fight in the war, you asked me to write it, so I did. I am sorry, but no one wants to read such a horrible story. I can assure you as someone who was there, it's not to be fantasized as a heroic battle between men fighting for their countries. It was nothing but men killing other men because the men in a higher place said so."

"Well write that, we can't accept this."

"So, you won't put it in the paper?"

"No, it is not acceptable"

"What about the bonus?" he looked at me sympathetically, "since you did the work, you're entitled to it, but I would still like another piece, we'll put it in next week," I was devastated that he didn't want it but I was relieved he still gave me the bonus.

When I went back to Oliver and Mary's home, I gave it to Oliver to read since he pushed me so hard to start writing again anyway. He loved it. "I can't believe they don't want to put this in the paper it's amazing."
"Yes, well they disagree" I said dully "Idiots, honestly. Maybe you should try to get this published yourself?"
"What's the point? No one likes it but you and it's too short,"
"You have only showed two people Sam, and you could easily make this longer if the publisher wants it that way,"
"Well fifty percent of those people don't like it, I don't know if I like it anymore, it's a bit childish. Maybe people do want to hear about the true horrors of war. Maybe that's what my son will grow up reading. I wonder how he will view me then? How much worse can he think of me? But I got the bonus, that's all I really wanted,"
"Don't be silly. Get it published and then you can bring that back to Claudia. People need to escape sometimes. And I know some veterans who will want this kind of escape."
"Like whom?"
"John."
"You're still in contact with John?"
"Of course I am. He writes to me every week. He hasn't left his house since he got back though,"
"I don't blame him."
"Here's an idea. You make this longer, then send a copy to a publishing house and I'll send one to John?" I nodded and then got to work on making the short story a novel.

I worked day after day until finally I had a full novel that I was proud of. Oliver took it to his work and made two copies of it, one I took to a publishing house in

London and the other Oliver read before sending it to John. Once he completed the full manuscript he sung its praise to me and Mary, "It's fantastic Mary, once it's published we'll get another copy," Mary looked at me and smiled, I think she saw how dedicated I was to getting back to my family. "When will you hear back from the publishing house?" Oliver asked me eagerly, "I'm not sure, but they might not like it," I replied, "nonsense. It was amazing Sam." He was wrong, it was rejected four times before finally someone liked it. I would have given up if it weren't for Oliver pushing me to keep trying and John's feedback. The fifth publishing company wrote me a letter that thanked me for choosing them to publish "such a master piece", they said that it was a story that needed to be told and depicted the truth of life in the trenches, something John also praised it for. Alongside the letter they sent me a cheque. I was so excited so when I got it, I immediately showed it to Oliver who congratulate me over and over, "well-done Sam, I told you someone would pick it up!" this was the only time I didn't mind being told I was wrong. "You should tell Claudia," he said enthusiastically, "go now and come get your stuff later. I'm sure she's going to be so happy for you" "Thank you Oliver, I should go now, before Bart's dinner," I replied and grabbed my coat and got ready to go, "wait, I have to tell Mary," he ran out of the study and I went with him downstairs, Mary congratulated me and they both hugged me and wished me luck at the front door. I put the cheque in my pocket and kept a grip of it to keep it safe and then I was off to win back my wife.

I knocked confidently but as I waited for an answer my nerves sunk into my chest and I felt my heart getting faster and faster, then she answered, "Hello, Claudia," I said with a big smile, but for some reason I wasn't expecting the cold greeting I received, "What on earth are you doing here?" she asked coldly, "I got a new job and I have a book that's going to be published," I replied hold out my cheque to her, "you may have all of that but that doesn't prove anything. Not much has changed has its Sam?"

"Claudia please, it has. It will. The only thing I want in my life is to have my son and my wife back, please will you forgive me?" even angry she was beautiful, and I found myself getting lost in her eyes once again, "Sam, I did forgive you. And then you got worse. I understand you have been through a lot, but I am not equipped to help you, and Bart doesn't deserve a dad who isn't going to show him the right way in life. Do you want him falling into the same pattern it seems you and your own dad did?"

"But Claudia, I'm getting better, I wrote a story, I'm back to my old self again."

"I don't believe you; I can't believe you; you look horrible. You're wasting away Samuel and you did it all alone. How can you expect me to help you when you don't want to help yourself?"

"Claudia please-"

"Goodbye Sam,"

"Well at least take the money. Please, for Bart."

"We already have plenty of your money Sam so please leave now." she slammed the door in my face. That was the last time I will see my wife and my son.

I felt like my heart had been ripped out of my chest and tossed away right in front of me. I was too ashamed to go back to Oliver's, but I also felt like he betrayed me by getting my hopes up, so I wondered the streets until I decided finally to go to the pub. There I drank myself to black, as you can probably imagine. Once again, I told all of the other drunks about the tragedy that is my life. I didn't stop drinking until I couldn't walk. And the only reason I did that was because when I stood up, I fell straight back down and ended up on the pub floor. The next thing I remember is waking up once again here in this hospital. Wasting away slowly. With no one but my loyal friend whose kindness I am utterly undeserving of. The doctors don't know what the matter is with me. And with the Spanish Flu epidemic they don't have the time or resources to spend on figuring it out. All they can do is pump me full of medication they think will help and pray, but I know I'm on my way out regardless of the hope they maintain.

How does one manage to survive war when I couldn't survive a heartbreak? How did I manage to lose everyone but the naively faithful man that I call my brother? I was so absorbed into becoming a better man than my dad and achieving all he couldn't that I ended up becoming him instead. There is no more suiting word for what I am other than pathetic, I am pathetic. I wasted my life to please others and it turned me into everything I have ever hated. I resent man. I resent myself because I resent man. My life meant something and now I have wasted it and it's too late to change.

Printed in Great Britain
by Amazon